Lechuza

Eerie And Unusual True Tales

by

Hernán Moreno Hinojosa

Lechuza

Hope Kelley Book Publishing

www.HopeKelleyBookPublishing.com

800.806.6240

Printed in the United States of America

ISBN 9780578725352

ISBN 978-0-578-72535-2
51499

9 780578 725352

2

Lechuza

Lechuza

Lechuza

Table of Contents

Lechuza

Lechuza

Dedication

*First, I wish to thank God who makes all things possible.
Thank you to my wonderful family who always has my back.*

*I also dedicate this book to Saint Michael the Archangel,
Patron Saint, and protector of Law Enforcement Officers.*

*And finally, to the Houston Metro Police Officers honored at
the end of this book, who have died or have been killed since
1996.*

*Not all the officers remembered and honored died directly in
the line-of-duty. None-the-less, law enforcement is extremely
stressful. And so, even if some of these brave individuals died
peacefully in their sleep, which is the best that any of us can
hope for, or if they died of some lingering malady, or of a
sudden stroke or heart attack, it is safe to assume that the
stress of their daily work shortened their life spans to some
degree. And so, thank you one and all for your service.
Requiescat in Pace...*

~~ Hernán Moreno Hinojosa

Lechuza

Foreword

Hernán Moreno Hinojosa is a marvelous storyteller. He is also our Father. We grew up hearing his tales, most we believed, some we could not... but we knew our father to be an honest man, so we always gave him the benefit of the doubt.

Huddled around listening to his stories on cold and rainy evenings will always be special memories for all of us. Wonderfully excited to hear our father's stories again in this collection of tales.

~~ Marissa, Fernando, Stela Marie, and Diana

Lechuza

Prologue

Hernán Moreno Hinojosa is a retired Law Enforcement Officer and Author. Hernán became interested in collecting folk stories when he was only 16, and still living in Hebbronville, Texas with his parents, the late Tito Moreno and Maria Moreno-Hinojosa.

Hernán would frequently accompany his father to La Florida Ranch, which was leased for cattle production at the time. Most ghost stories about La Florida Ranch were told by word-of-mouth. Strangely enough, no one would remain at La Florida after dark. One of the employees told Hernán, "This place has many ghosts that we leave as soon as the sun begins to set."

The ghost most frequently mentioned at La Florida was Candelaria, a 17-year-old girl who was said committed suicide by drowning and believed to still haunt the ranch. One night, Hernán found Candelaria's lost grave and immediately realized that the story of Candelaria was not a legend. Candelaria was a real-live person who lived and died during the mid-1800's. Hernán realized her story had to be recorded before it became just another *Cuento Viejo*, or legend. *If the story of Candelaria is true, what about the other ghost stories frequently repeated by the older generations?*

11

Hernán began writing down all these stories.
The story of Candelaria was first published in
1994, by *TEXAS Sunday Magazine* of the *Houston
Chronicle Newspaper.* Hernán was already a
Metro Policeman, and Houstonians begin calling
Hernán at work and leaving messages; *"I am a
teacher in the City of South Houston. Can you come
and speak to my class? I think I am related to
Candelaria. Can you tell me where her grave is?
Would you like to join our writer's group?"*

Hernán submitted a 24-story manuscript to
*Piñata Books (University of Houston Arté Publico
Press)*. Half of the stories were approved by *Piñata
Books*, published, and released under the title of
The Ghostly Rider.
The rest of the stories were later accepted by
Overlooked Books and published, and by the
Valley Byliners who featured eight of his stories in
two anthologies they published.

Hernán retired from the Metro Police in 2008. He
currently divides his time between their Houston
home and their South Texas ranch with his wife,
Herlinda Garza. They recently celebrated their
48th wedding anniversary. They are blessed with
four children: three girls, one son, and one
grandson. He is still collecting ghost stories and
writing. Sit back and enjoy reading these tales!

Chapter 1

Persona Non-Grata

The unique and wonderful thing about life, is that we do not know where it will lead us. I grew up in a small town in South Texas situated south of San Antonio, north of the *magic Rio Grande Valley*, east of the *Streets of Laredo*, and west of the *City of the Body of Christ*. Once I graduated from the local high school in Hebbronville in 1967, I traveled south into the Rio Grande Valley to seek my fortune. As fate would have it, I was hired on nearly immediately with a local municipal police department as a police dispatcher. In those days, which I fondly remember as the "dark days of law enforcement," a favorable interview with the Chief of Police would suffice to gain one admission into the local police force.

In other words, your employment with municipal law enforcement was at the pleasure of the local Chief of Police. There were no background checks to speak of, no drug screenings, no physicals, no polygraph test, and no firearm qualifications. There were, however, only height and weight requirements.

The reason for the height and weight requirements was very practical. There were no special charges to be brought against a person who just happened to beat-up a police officer. It was as if two thugs just decided to punch each other out. If the police officer wanted to arrest someone, he had to be tougher than the bad guy. Of course, the officer did carry a .38 Special at the time, but it could easily be lost in a scuffle. Double and triple retention holsters were not yet the norm. A simple leather strap snapped over the pistol's hammer precariously held the officer's revolver in his holster. So, it was important that the bad guy did not have a significant size and weight advantage over the officer.

Minimum height requirements in those days were 5'10" and minimum weight of 150 pounds. I then only stood at 5' 9," and I only weighed 120 pounds soaking wet.

Not wanting to remain a police dispatcher my entire career, I started lifting weights daily, and soon I tipped the scale at 135 lbs. I gained five inches across my chest, which made me appear bulkier, if not heavier. I took to wearing black cowboy boots with a pronounced heel which gave me nearly a two-inch advantage. Now I appeared to meet the height and weight requirements. No one was going to take a tape measure and check my height, nor ask me to step on a scale. The seemingly impossible height and weight requirements were easily achieved with just a little stealth.

As a point of interest, I did mention that firearms qualifications were not required for police officers then. Even though my immediate position did not necessitate that I carry a handgun, it was assumed that I would eventually become a patrol officer. The matter of carrying a handgun was mandatory for patrol officers.

The firearms requirements were remarkably simple: A Colt or Smith & Wesson revolver in .38 Special or .357 Magnum (loaded with .38 Special ammunition), preferably in blue steel finish rather than nickel plated. Stainless steel was not yet available for handguns and bright nickel was frowned upon because common wisdom dictated that a shiny handgun would only serve to give the officer's position away in the event of a gunfight. Not that gunfights were an everyday occurrence. That is a fallacy perpetuated by Hollywood, the Silver Screen, and the then popular paperback crime novels.

The standard question posed to the new patrolman was, "Do you own a .38 or .357 Magnum revolver?" Revolver was specified because again, conventional wisdom dictated that an automatic, or more correctly, an auto-loading handgun was inherently prone to jam.

15

If the officer replied, "Yes, I do own a revolver," the following question was, "Is it a Colt or Smith & Wesson with at least a four-inch barrel?"

Colt and Smith & Wesson were specified because other brands were considered unreliable. Wrong or right, these were the accepted police revolvers during this time.

If the new police officer replied, "No, I do not own a handgun," the matter was simply corrected by providing the new officer with a department issued loaner until he could save enough money to purchase his own revolver. It is probably worthy of mention that no aspiring Texas policeman was asked if he knew how to use a revolver. I suppose that it was assumed that all Texas men could just naturally shoot proficiently! Small wonder that I fondly recall these days as, *the dark days of Law Enforcement.*" Although, I cannot be certain, not all police officers were *believers*. Evidenced by the survival of so many of us then and now, the Grace of God was actively involved.

By the 1990's, we were living in an enlightened age of Law Enforcement. In fact, as early as 1969, TCLEOSE (Texas Commission on Law Enforcement Standards and Education, which was formed in 1965), set the standard for Texas

Peace Officers. Later, on January 1st of 2014, TCLEOSE became TCOLE (Texas Commission on Law Enforcement).

Since I had taken a long Sabbatical from law enforcement from approximately 1972, until 1990, I learned that now, due to the new rulings, I would have to attend the Police Academy to return to law enforcement. Fortunately, Gilbert Ybañez, the Sheriff of Jim Hogg County, Texas, was willing to sponsor me through the Academy. Without a law enforcement agency sponsoring me, I would have to pay for the academy out of my own pocket. Being unemployed at the time, this was not a viable option. The only real downside was that soon I would turn 42, and the academy I was scheduled to attend was held during the heat of summer, in Laredo, Texas. El Paso and Laredo have long vied for the dubious honor of the hottest city in Texas!

Along with some other cadets sponsored by the Jim Hogg County Sheriff's Office, we showed up at the Laredo Regional Police Academy to apply as cadets. The director of the Police Academy looked at me appraisingly and asked me, "How old are you?"

"Forty-two, sir," was my terse reply.

"And you think you can complete the academy?" He continued, "The average age of the attending

17

cadets is twenty-one. Half of them will not complete the Academy. You are twice their age and you think you can graduate?"

"*No viene a ver si puedo. Viene porque puedo* — I am not here to try. I'm here because I *can* graduate your Academy, sir."

The first day of the Academy, I showed up wearing a polo shirt, blue jeans, ball cap and Red Wing® steel-toe boots. At four pm, we were ordered to change into our gym clothes and report for PT (physical training). I reported to PT in a polo shirt, blue jeans, ball cap and steel-toe boots.

The PT instructor pointed at me saying in a strong, loud voice, "You, hurry up and get into your PT clothes."

"Sir," I asked, "what are we going to do for PT?" He promptly replied, "We are going to run two-and-a-half miles. Hurry up and get ready."

"Sir," I insisted, "I'm running like this; if I have to run after a bad guy, do you think he's going to give me time to change into my jogging outfit?"

Mr. Acosta, the PT instructor, glared at me saying, "Okay wise guy, try to keep up."

I took my position directly behind Mr. Acosta. We started at an easy jog and slowly increased our pace. The instructor kept looking back, surprised somewhat, that each time he checked, I was maintaining my position behind him.

Eleven cadets failed to complete the run that afternoon. The first seven to drop out were twenty-one years old. At the end of the track I asked our PT instructor if we were going to do anything else that afternoon?

He said, "That's all. You did good cadet. Go home and get some rest."

The rest of the cadets nicknamed me 'grandpa,' but no one ever suggested that I would not finish the academy after that afternoon.

Although I successfully completed the Academy, due to a hiring freeze, I did not hire on with the Jim Hogg County Sheriff's Office. Sheriff Ybañez suggested that I apply for work with the Laredo Police Academy as a Campus Cop. The Chief of the Campus Police was none other than the director of the Laredo Regional Police Academy. He was pleased to welcome me onboard as a Campus Cop.

In 1992, a large east Texas, Metropolitan Police Department was in Laredo recruiting bilingual police officers. By this time, I had worked as a Campus Police Officer for a little longer than a year. The job fair was hosted by the Laredo Junior College.

I was at the job fair on campus that day, looking for a Police Officer friend of mine, Gabriel Garcia, to see if he had made plans for lunch. The job fair was crowded. Many Police agencies were present recruiting. The age-ceiling for new police officers was 35 years of age. I was past that age, so I was not too enthused about hiring on with a different department.

I noticed a job fair booth with the signage, "Metro Police." I wondered what a Metro Police Department was, and how it differed from a municipal police department? A uniformed Police Officer rose from his place in this booth and walked toward me. I noticed that he wore lieutenant's bars on his collar.

"Excuse me Officer," he stated, "Do you trade police patches?"

"No Lieutenant," I replied, "I do not, but my Sergeant does."

He introduced himself as Inspector Ron Willes, elaborating that his official title was '*inspector*,' a rank like that of a police lieutenant, and that he liked my uniform patch. He was wondering if my

Sergeant was available to see him about trading patches.

"Yes sir, Inspector," I replied, "he is in his office doing paperwork. I am sure he will see you. Why don't you walk with me to my patrol car? I'll take you to the station and arrange an introduction."

Walking over to my patrol car Inspector Willes casually asked me if I was Hispanic. I nodded in affirmation.

"And are you bilingual?" he inquired.

"I am," I replied. "I speak, read and write English and Spanish, and I can interpret or translate either language." Interpretation is an oral rending of one language into another; translation is written.

As we sat in my patrol car and I fired up the engine and the air conditioning, the Inspector continued, "We are actually here to recruit bilingual officers. Are you interested?"

Going into his recruiting mode, he elaborated, "The Metro Police is based in Houston, Texas. We have jurisdiction in the City of Houston, Harris County, Fort Bend County, Waller, and Montgomery Counties. Only DPS (Texas Department of Public Safety, the Texas Highway

Patrol) has more ordinary jurisdiction than we do. Are you ready for a change, Officer?"

"Well, maybe." I answered somewhat tenuously, "I am older than 35, and you probably have an age ceiling?"

"No Officer, we don't have an age ceiling provided that you can pass the written exam, physical agility, drug screening, psychological screening and the polygraph test." He continued, "I won't lie to you Officer, the job is dangerous, but if you're interested, I'm sure I can offer you more pay than what you are earning right now. We will provide you with all your equipment; uniform, gun, gun belt, bullet proof vest, even boots if you require them. The only thing we won't provide for you is underwear."

Bullet proof vest? Our department could not afford ballistic vests. To my knowledge, the only officers in Laredo who wore ballistic vests were the ones who could afford to purchase their own. This excluded all Campus Police Officers in our department.

"Inspector, I own my own revolver—"

"That Colt Python you are carrying? You can leave it in Laredo. In Houston, you will need more than six rounds." The Inspector sounded serious.

I know I frowned when I asked, "What about the Police Academy?" The last thing I wanted to do was go through another Police Academy.

"You are already a Texas Peace Officer," he answered, "we are not going to insult you by making you go through another academy. We need officers on patrol now. You will go through a field training program, but that is not difficult. So, what do you say?" The Inspector could not have known that he had offered me an annual $11,000 more starting salary than my current salary. Or perhaps he did know! My only question was, "When can I start?"

I could not believe how quickly things moved along after that. The most difficult part of the field training program for me was city orientation. Houston is the largest city in Texas and the fourth largest city in the Nation. To a country boy like me, Laredo was a big City. Houston was unbelievably huge. Fortunately for me, most of my fellow rookie officers were from the Houston area and they went out of their way to help me navigate around the City of Houston, and the surrounding areas within our jurisdiction. It made not one Iota of difference if they were White, Black, Hispanic, or Asian. We all bled blue and we were all brothers-in-arms, and brothers-in-blue.

Lechuza

Two weeks into my new job as a Metro Policeman, our Sergeant asked me to have lunch with him. We sat down at a popular burger joint and began to converse.

 "I do this with all my new officers," Sgt. Emilio Ruiz began, "I like to get to know my men, one-on-one, and I always ask them this question, so don't take it personally. Do you believe in God?"

The question caught me off guard. Of course, the Sergeant would ask. We are in a dangerous profession.

I made eye-contact with Sgt. Ruiz, "Sergeant, if I did not believe in God, I could not be a police officer here, back in Laredo, or anywhere else."

All the Sergeant said was, "Good." After some more light conversation, we finished our burgers, returned to our respective patrol cars, and resumed patrolling.

Due to our work schedule, every Wednesday we had two platoons working on evening shift. We would take turns working freeway management and downtown patrol. One Wednesday, one platoon would work the freeways and the other platoon would work some specialized assignment downtown. These specialized assignments were usually plain-clothes, or what is sometimes called, *undercover assignments*.

One Wednesday evening, I was assigned to a plain clothes detail in an unmarked, dark blue police van, with four other Metro Police Officers. Our orders were to concentrate on drug arrests and vice, and we were assigned to work the Montrose area of downtown Houston.

Montrose is not like other neighborhoods. There is a concentration of unseemly and weird denizens who gravitate to the Montrose area whenever the moon is full, and even when it is not full. I had already worked this area before and one almost becomes accustomed to seeing men made-up and dressed like women, and women dressed and made-up like men, walking around in plain view. Even so, nothing could have prepared me for what I would encounter that dark night. No amount of police training could have prepared me for this strange, chance encounter. How could I know that before this night ended, I was destined to come face-to-face with the most reviled and infamous villain in our entire human history?

As we approached the intersection of Montrose Blvd. and West Main, we noticed a large, white male lying on his back in the moving lane of traffic. It seemed that he had attempted to cross Montrose Blvd. from west to east, and made it to

25

the island separating the north and southbound lanes of Montrose Blvd. There he must have slipped, landed flat on his back and he was obviously unable to get back up. We were southbound, and he was on the northbound moving-lane-of-traffic. We had to hurry and turn around to get on the northbound lanes before some careless driver accidently ran over him.

We could not use the van's emergency lights (which were concealed behind the grill and the red taillight lenses) without exposing ourselves as undercover police officers. Greg Johnson, the driver, stopped right in front of the downed man with his four-way flashers on. Along with the other three available officers, I got down and hurried toward the man on the roadway.

He appeared not to be seriously injured. Rapidly we grabbed the big man by a hand and ankle and carried him back to the corner convenience store on the west side of Montrose Blvd. We propped him against the wall of the convenience store and turned to return to our assignment.

The old timer appeared to be a street person, even though he did not reek like a person who had been living on the streets and who had not bathed in days. His clothes were old but clean and in good condition. He did not appear to be inebriated and so we turned to leave.

Lechuza

As we left, he called out to us in a cheerful voice, "Thank you boys, I'm Judas."

I half-turned over my right shoulder to answer him, "Nice to meet you Jude. See you later—"

My skin broke out in goose-flesh when he replied in an unbelievably bitter voice, "I'm not Thaddaeus. I am Judas Iscariot, the Traitor."

How many people, even in a place as large as Houston, could possibly know that St. Jude the Apostle, Saint, and near-kinsman of the Lord, was Thaddaeus, Judas Thaddaeus? I froze in my tracks.

"Come here young man," he insisted, "I want to show you something."

Young man? When this happened, I was fifty years old. Half-a-Century old and he referred to me as a young man? Of course, if he were the person he claimed to be, he would be more than 2,000 years old! He most certainly could call me, *young man*.

I stood motionlessly, still somewhat stunned by what had just transpired. "Come here," Judas spoke in the imperative. I shambled slowly toward him like a zombie. Time seemed to cease. In fact, I marveled that my fellow policemen were not shouting at me to hurry up and get back into the van.

Judas reached into his right shirt pocket and retrieved a small notebook. He handed the notebook to me saying, "They sent me back..."

"They?"

"*They Who Are One* sent me back, to write down everything that is happening now, because we *are* in the Last Days. And see, I have been keeping a faithful record!"

This was rapidly becoming entirely too bizarre for me. I took his notebook and I opened it. To my astonishment the words appeared to be ancient Aramaic, a language that is older than the Bible. Did Judas know that I would recognize, albeit not be able to read this script? A friend of mine who is a Franciscan Priest once showed me a New Testament that was printed in Aramaic. The calligraphy seemed identical. There before my astonished eyes, were page after page of the tight, superbly written cursive in the notebook Judas Iscariot was showing me.

Reverently I returned the notebook to Judas and handed him a single dollar. He thanked me and promptly fell asleep leaning on the wall of that store we had propped him against.

I rejoined my friends in the van as if not a moment had passed. Indeed, my friends did not seem to miss me, nor did they ask me why I had taken so long returning to the van. We never spoke of that incident, and for years I never did tell anyone of the night that I came face-to-face with the man who betrayed our Lord Jesus Christ for the price of a slave, thirty pieces of silver.

Was Judas simply mad, or was he perhaps serving some yet undisclosed purpose in the history of Christendom? In any case, even though I occasionally returned to Montrose, I never did see, nor did I hear from Judas again. Could it be that even in a place as unusual as Montrose, Judas Iscariot was unwelcome, a pariah, a *persona non-grata* condemned to wander the Earth until the Second Coming? This is a question that I can only answer with another question, *quien sabe*, who knows? Some things are not for us to know.

Lechuza

Chapter 2

The Last Dance

In South Texas, you still hear people tell this story. It is quite old and is told nearly as frequently as the one about *La Llorona*.

Most people agree that the name of the protagonist of our story was Cristina—or I should say, her name *is* Cristina, because if the story is to be believed, she still lives, but I am getting ahead of myself.

Cristina lived in Laredo, on the Texas side of the border, with her widowed mother. Every Saturday night Cristina could be found at the VFW Hall, *en el baile, (the dance)*. Undeniably, the prettiest girl present, and a superb dancer, all the boys stood in line for a chance to dance at least one dance with Cristina. Those who were not fortunate enough to dance with her were thrilled to see her dance. Her long, silky black hair flowed through the air with the rhythm of the music. Her big brown, mischievous and lively eyes, and her alabaster skin, like that of a doll of finest porcelain, fascinated them.

Cristina was very vain. She knew she was beautiful, and she could be cruel and haughty. As Cristina became older, and even more beautiful, she was more selective about her dance partners. She threw her chin up and refused to dance with many of her former dance partners and classmates. Besides being too young, and immature, she would rationalize; they have no future and no chance to become men of wealth.

That Saturday night some forty years ago, Cristina's mother asked her to stay home, "Cristina, *mija,*" her mother implored, "Please don't go to the dance tonight. I am not feeling well, and you should stay home in case I get sick during the night. You may have to go after the doctor."

Doctors still made house calls in those days, but there was no telephone in Cristina's house. They were much too poor for such a luxury. Cristina would have to walk over to the neighbor's house and use their telephone to call the doctor should her mother require medical attention during the night.

"Mama," Cristina said with a sly smile, "do not worry, I shall stay home tonight. If you feel sick during the night, just call out to me, Mama, and I will run over to the neighbor's house to call the doctor for you."

Cristina had no intention of missing the Saturday night dance. Her mother was just being silly; there was nothing wrong with her. Her heart, her mother would say, but Cristina knew that there was really nothing wrong with her mother. She was healthy as a horse and she was just jealous of Cristina, because she was too old to go out and have a good time.

After supper Cristina waited for her mother to go to bed. "Mama," she said, "it is already getting dark. Why don't you go to bed early Mama, so that you will feel better in the morning?"

"Cristina," her mother said with a tinge of fear in her voice, "stay home tonight. I am really afraid that if you are not with me to go for the doctor, I will not live through the night."

Cristina smiled at her aged mother. She had become so helpless and silly since Father died. She pretended to be afraid of everything only so that Cristina could lavish attention on her. Just a year ago her father died of a heart attack, and now her mother was so sure that her own heart would fail her.

33

Lechuza

"You have to let him go, Mama," Cristina would tell her mother, "The dead are dead, and the living must go on living and enjoying life. That is why you feel so sick all the time, Mama."

"No *mija*," her mother would reply, "I am really sick from my heart."

"Mama, Dr. Mata comes over, checks your heart, and tells you not to worry so much. He won't even prescribe medicine for you."

"*Mija*, we cannot afford the doctor's medicine. The welfare checks we spend goes to groceries, rent, new shoes, and clothes for you to wear. Now that you are almost out of high school you should think of finding work to help us out."

"Mama, I will not work. I am going to find a rich man to marry so that he will take care of me. You will see."

"Do not say such things, *mija*, girls should only marry for love, not for money."

"Mama, I do not want to live the way we do. You married *papa* for love and see where it got us. I do not want to marry a man who will work himself to death and leave me with a meager welfare check to raise a child. No, Mama, I shall find a wealthy man to marry. You will see."

Lechuza

That night, after Cristina's mother went to bed, Cristina only waited long enough for her mother to fall asleep. When she knew that her mother would be sound asleep, she slipped out the back door to walk the short distance to the VFW Hall as she did every Saturday night. But, unlike many other nights, tonight the moon seemed larger than usual, casting a bright, eerie silvery glow. Cristina walked through the well-lit path. She looked up as if to thank the moon; the moon shone on her with a bright, sinister-like smile.

A few blocks from her house she walked past a vacant lot. A shrill wolf-whistle echoed from the shadows, "*Wheeew, whew...*"

The street was deserted, as was the vacant lot. Cristina hesitated. "*Wheeew, whew,*" the shrill call came again.

Nervously, Cristina looked all around. Men whistled at her like that, but never at night and never from the dark. Who could be whistling at her now?

"Wheeew, whew..." the shrill sound came from the vacant lot. Now Cristina sighted a *lechuza* perched on the gnarled limb of an old mesquite tree that grew right in the middle of that vacant lot. From its perch the owl's two large, piercing yellow eyes stared right at her as if staring into her very soul.

"*Lechuzas* are just owls," her father would tell her when she was little, but her grandmother insisted that they were really witches that took the form of owls. Cristina signed herself with the holy sign. Immediately a huge Horned Owl extended its enormous wings and launched into the air. Cristina hurried off. Soon she noticed that a dark shadow seemed to pace her. Was the lezucha following her, or was it just her imagination?

As Cristina neared the dancehall, she could hear the merry music, the kind of music that would ease her conscience. Walking through the parking lot Cristina stared with disdain at the same old pickup trucks and jalopies that the local boys drove to the dance. Wait, there in the very front, a sleek, black brand-new Cadillac car. Cristina's heart raced. Her dreams were about to come true. Only a truly wealthy man could afford to come to the dance in such a nice car. If only she could find him and dance with him, he would become convinced to take her for his wife.

All eyes were on Cristina as she walked through the door in her favorite red dress. She turned down every offer to dance wondering where the owner of the new car could be.

Lechuza

Just before midnight, when it appeared that Cristina would not dance that night, the crowd parted as a tall, dark handsome stranger walked straight toward her. The dance hall fell silent as the dark stranger walked up to Cristina, holding out his hand in supplication to dance that very last dance with him.

The band began to play and Cristina and the handsome stranger, all dressed in black to match his Cadillac, took to the center of the dance floor and began to dance. They had the entire dance floor to themselves, as no other couple dared to step in beat with them. There was something ominous about the handsome stranger. The others decided to sit that last dance out and watch the two whirling across the dance floor together.

The handsome stranger was even better on the dance floor than Cristina and soon she found herself out of breath trying to keep up with the stranger's rapid, graceful moves. He moved like a cat across the dance floor, gliding rapidly and gracefully along the floor with Cristiana in tow. He spun, dipped, dove, and pirouetted in a savage frenzy all but dragging Cristina after him.

Suddenly Cristina's mind drifted back home to her sick mother. *She needs me*, Cristina thought, but the stranger was not finished dancing. Cristina tried to pull away, to run home to her mother, but the stranger held her fast, moving in frenzied time to the beat of the music.

The music reached its crescendo and the stranger stood motionless, pulling Cristina closer, his left hand flat on her back. Suddenly the mood shifted. It was, as if it were possible, that the entire dance hall was now somehow closer to Hell?

The crowd let out a collective gasp as a strange odor waft through the air. It was the stench of brimstone and burning sulfur that filled the stifled atmosphere. All at once every soul rushed for the door leaving Cristina and the stranger alone on the dance floor. The band quit playing and, abandoning their instruments, they too scrambled for the door.

With cold, black eyes the stranger stared deeply into Cristina's eyes. His smile curled into a sneer as he drew her even closer. Cristina closed her eyes as the stranger kissed her. After a moment Cristina broke free of his embrace, she turned and raced out the door.

Cristina ran all the way home finally stumbling into her dark house. "Mama," Cristina cried out, "Mama."

 "Mama," she called a third time stepping into her mother's bedroom.

It was too late. Cristina's mother lay dead in her bed, her body already cold.

"MAMA!" Cristina screamed, running into the bathroom. Cristina looked in the bathroom mirror and collapsed.

The following Monday, around noon, José Manuel, the high school truancy officer, knocked on Cristina's front door. There was no answer and so he called the local Sheriff's Office from the neighbor's house.

Sheriff Rivera joined the truancy officer at Cristina's house. "I do not like this,"

José Manuel explained, "only the screen door is latched, and a funny odor comes from the house. Also," he added nervously, "I keep hearing a strange keening sound from somewhere within."

Standing on the small front porch the Sheriff instructed José Manuel, "Wait here while I check inside." With a pocket knife the Sheriff unlatched the screen door. Moments later he returned pale as ghost, his Stetson hat in his left hand, a red bandana held in his right hand over his nose and mouth. He coughed and said, "The old lady is days dead. The girl is in the bathroom lamenting her mother's death."

"José," the Sheriff said suddenly, "go to the neighbor's house and use their telephone to call for an ambulance. Perhaps Dr. Mata can still help the girl."

But even the good doctor could not help Cristina. She was completely out of her mind.

"Grief," Dr. Mata explained, "she lost her mind from grief. First, she lost her father, then, a year later, her mother. It was too much for the young girl to bear."

To this very day, it is said that Cristina resides in Ward H of the State Insane Asylum on South Presa St. in San Antonio, Texas. The letter 'H' is for... *Hopeless*.

Cristina never has any visitors. Even the residents avoid her. They believe that Cristina has been marked. Indeed, no one can explain the strange burn marks on Cristina's back or her seared lips. People who were there that night say that Cristina danced that last dance with no less a personage than the Devil himself. It was he, they say, who marked Cristina for his very own.

Chapter 3

The Airplane Crash That Never Happened

During the late 1980s, an airplane dropped out of
the cold night sky in Jim Hogg County, Texas. The
plane skidded to a stop on a private 200 acre
ranch which goes from Hebbronville to Realitos,
Texas on the east side of town. According to my
sources, (who shall remain unnamed), the landing
gear of this airplane snagged on a gnarled
Mesquite stump and the airplane flipped belly-up.

According to these same sources, person-or-
persons unknown, under the cover of darkness,
cut a barb-wire fence and accessed the airplane
from Texas 359 highway. These unknown persons
backed a pickup truck to the crashed airplane. I,
of course, posed the following question, "What was
taken from the airplane?"

"The seats," was the concise reply.

A few days later, a sizable twin-prop airplane,
appeared in a vacant lot catty-corner to where
there now is, the only Valero/Stripes gas station
and convenience store in Hebbronville. The
airplane was a beautiful beige color and had all
the appearances of a luxury aircraft. It was similar
to the Cessna T-50 'Bobcat,' except that this

airplane had five or six round port-hole windows along the fuselage.

Again, I posed a question to my confidential source, "How did the airplane get into town?"

"It was transported to the present location from the crash site by a flat-bed trailer." Before my source could wander off, I asked, "How was it loaded onto the flatbed trailer?"

My source looked back at me over his left shoulder and answered, "The authorities borrowed some heavy equipment from a local oil and gas company."

When this airplane was dropped off in the vacant lot, I lived thirteen miles west of Hebbronville, TX. in the town of Bruni. I drove into Hebbronville two or three times a week by way of SH-359, (regionally known as the *Laredo Highway*), on the west side of town. This route is well-traveled by the local citizenry, and during the four or five weeks that the airplane sat there, it must have been seen by the locals hundreds of times. Why is it now, after inquiring of many, that I am the only one who remembers this airplane?

One day, I stopped in the vacant lot and walked around the airplane. Close-up it looked huge. Without a ladder it was impossible for me to peer through any of the half-dozen porthole windows along the length of the fuselage. I did, however, stand right in front of one of the radial engines.

42

Lechuza

I stood front-and-center to the engine and reached up with both arms to see if I could touch the top of the engine cowling. Standing on my tiptoes I could barely touch the upper lip of the engine cowling with my fingertips. The chromed tri-vane propellers were bent back.

With millions of acres of flatlands in South Texas, what would possess an experienced pilot to attempt to land this big bird on a ranch less than two-hundred acres in size? Small jet planes landed at the local county airport during hunting season all the time, why not this slower moving prop-job airplane? Was he afraid of running out of runway, or was it something else that he feared?

When I next ran into my friend, I asked him if he knew who owned this big airplane? He replied, "It is registered to some bank in San Antonio."

I did not see a registration number on the airplane's side. Perhaps the custom paint job had concealed the numeration, or perhaps the numbers appeared underneath the wings. The landing gear was either retracted or removed, and the plane sat flat on its belly.

The larger mystery, as far as I am concerned, is why the entire local populous appears to have developed mass-amnesia concerning this crash, and the presence of this airplane in what then was known as the four-corners area of town? Amnesia is not as common as bad mystery plots would have us believe. True amnesia occurs after a severe head injury, or some kind of dementia. Mass amnesia is probably a medical/scientific impossibility. Yet, none of my friends appear to remember seeing this airplane in the vacant lot. When I bring this subject up with friends who were living in Hebbronville when this airplane crashed, they will: 1). Change the subject; 2). Flat-out say they do not remember or, 3). Say, they must have been living elsewhere when it happened.

It is not like we see big, beige, twin-engine airplanes on the ground every day. And my attempts to Google this airplane crash does not yield any results. Allowing that I did not imagine the entire episode, with lurid details, mass-amnesia appears to be the only explanation.

One more incident worth mentioning, I was speaking last Sunday with a brother-in-law in the Valley, and I mentioned the entire story of *the airplane crash that never happened.* He pointed something out that completely evaded me back when I first heard of the plane crash.

Beto said, "The airplane seats were not removed. They were never there. They were already gone by the time the plane crashed."

"Of course," I remarked, embarrassed that it had not occurred to me before, "The seats were removed to make room for something else—

contraband such as drugs, laundered or counterfeited money, or possibly even smuggled humans."

"Exactly," Beto replied.

"Moot point though, *cuñado*. Even if this occurred as recently as 1989, it has been 30 years. The statues of limitations have likely already run out."

"The principals involved," Beto added, "are probably not even alive anymore. As far as mass-amnesia is concerned, that probably is a clinical impossibility, but selective-amnesia is real. Your friends probably just don't want to remember."

"That does make sense..."

Beto asked me, "What happened to your friend with all the answers?"

"He didn't even exist. At least, not as a real person. He was a literary device, a conglomeration of characters who told me the story. In the writing/publishing business, this is known as a *flat character*. He has no name, no background, and no history. His entire *raison d'être* is to provide information to help move the story along."

"Then this story is a work of fiction?"

"No," I replied shaking my head, "the story did happen, I'm just using a single fictive character to relate the entire story to me, rather than saying,

45

Lechuza

"Simple Simon told me this; John Doe said that; Juana la Cubana mentioned this."

This story closes but it does not end. It has no ending, only unanswered and perhaps unanswerable questions. Why did the pilot attempt to land in such a confined area? There is an old, abandoned runway in that area. It was primarily used by local pilots who flew private, one-engine Cessna airplanes, like the 152, and the 172. These airplanes are puny compared to the twin-prop behemoth that crashed here. A daytime landing attempt for an airplane that large was hazardous, but to attempt the landing during the dead-of-night was sheer lunacy. Did the big airplane simply run out of fuel, forcing the pilot to attempt a landing in such a reduced area?

The crashed airplane remained at the four-corners-area for weeks, but what became of the pilot and possible passengers or cargo? And who cut a barbed wire fence to back a pickup truck to the airplane? Under certain circumstances, it is still a felony in Texas (punishable by one to five years in prison), to cut a fence. So why would anyone risk prison time by cutting a fence to reach the downed airplane? To steal the airplane seats. How likely is that?

One possibility is that the pilot walked or hitched a ride into Hebbronville, the nearest town. Once there, the pilot could have made some telephone calls explaining the situation to the people that he worked for and asked for funds.

The pilot could have promised some of the local men a hundred dollars to assist him in removing the cargo.

"Just imports," the pilot probably explained, "Imports from Mexico or Colombia, nothing more." They would be helping a stranded pilot out and earning some spending cash for just a couple of hours of easy work.

However, what could explain the hysteria which resulted in a type of mass-amnesia? Perhaps word hit the streets that the Feds, rather than the local County Mounties, were handling the investigation into this airplane crash. Suddenly, nobody knew anything about a crashed airplane. Nobody cut a fence. Nobody backed a pickup truck to the crash site. And nobody helped the pilot unload cargo. Nobody saw any cargo, much less imports from Mexico or Columbia. In other words, *nobody left boot prints and fingerprints all over the crime scene and airplane,* because *nobody messed with a Federal Crime Scene!* In the interest of full-disclosure, I must add that, *some fool's partial fingerprints were on the upper lip of one of the engine's cowling.* One cannot help but wonder how those prints got there.

So, what happened? Not exactly mass-amnesia, but something like it. A conspiracy-of-silence induced by rumor-panic, *the Feds are coming, and they are going to put us all in jail!*

And so, the airplane crash, as if it were possible, was denied away. If nobody remembered it, then it just did not happen, *period.*

Chapter 4

The Open Window

Sometime, before the beginning of World War I, there lived a man outside of Bruni, Texas who did not like his son-in-law. This man lived in a two-story ranch house in Duval County, where a slice intrudes on both Webb and Jim Hogg Counties. Thus, leaving the question of county jurisdiction imprecise.

The reasons for his dislike of his son-in-law were not clear. Perhaps it was the eternal credence nurtured by a father that no man is good enough for his daughter. Or perhaps there were more specific reasons for his dislike of the young man.

Early one morning, while the son-in-law walked past his father-in-law's house, a shot rang out, shattering the early morning peace, and leaving the son-in-law dead.

The few witnesses present that morning, could not testify with any measure of certitude from where the rifle shot was fired. Nobody reported seeing a muzzle flash, nor a telltale signature smoke trail from the discharge.

The deputies from both Webb County, and the newly founded Jim Hogg County, agreed that the crime scene was actually in Duval County. Ironically, the county seat of Duval is further away than Jim Hogg or Webb Counties, and so the official investigation was delayed nearly a week. A deputy had to be sent for, and he came from the Duval County seat in San Diego, Texas.

In the meantime, Don Baltazar Romo, the father-in-law, tried to comfort his bereaved daughter and nearly immediately professed his innocence to anyone who would hear him. His profession of innocence was so noticeable, that it sent up red flags among the more astute.

Didn't Baltazar own one of those new .30 WCF, 1894 lever-action carbine guns with the nickel steel barrel? This was a rifle chambered for smoke-less ammunition which would certainly not leave a tell-tale smoke trail. The .30 WCF rifle is classified as a deer-rifle, but if such a rifle could kill a 200-pound Whitetail Deer, it could certainly kill a 180-pound man.

During the early 1900's, murder investigations were not an exact science. Law enforcement was a task for the toughest men who were willing to wear a tin star, tote a six-shooter, face some really bad *hombres*, and most importantly, be willing to work for a very minimal salary. Many lawmen were, at best, semi-literate, barely able to read and sign their own name, or count to ten.

The investigators were usually just the senior men on the force with nothing but experience, rather than investigative training, to qualify them for the prestigious rank of investigator. Forensics did not even come into the picture. Lifting and using fingerprints for identification was a science in its infancy. Even as early as 1686, a professor of anatomy at Bologna University in Italy, had noted that ridges, spirals, and loops in fingerprints differed from individual to individual. However, not much thought was given to using fingerprints for identification until 1856, when Magistrate Sir William Hershel started requiring natives of India to add their palm print to the back of contracts. This was to keep the natives from later repudiating their signatures.

During the time when Enrique Garcia, (Romo's son-in-law), met his untimely death, only the best organized and prestigious law enforcement agencies used modern methods to investigate crimes as vile as cold-blooded murder.

Had Garcia been a high-ranking *politico*, or a well-connected citizen, perhaps the Texas Rangers would have been called to investigate. The Rangers, however, were always busy pursuing bank robbers, horse thieves, train robbers, and cattle rustlers. They could not be bothered with investigating the low-profile murder of someone with a Mexican surname.

Wrong or right, the investigation was left to the
authorities of the County where the crime
occurred. And so, Deputy Adrian Canales from
Duval County, took nearly a week to arrive in
Bruni, Texas to initiate his investigation. Most of
the delay was waiting for a small advance on his
salary to pay for his room-and-board for two days.

Since Deputy Canales arrived late in the
afternoon, his first order of business was finding
room-and-board in the small community of Bruni.
A local widow had a room she could rent for fifty
cents a day. There were no hotel accommodations
in Bruni, but the room included breakfast and
coffee, and a light dinner included with price of
the rent. Breakfast and dinner both consisted of
eggs, any style, with potatoes, fried or baked, and
coffee or plain water. The menu was even more
reason for Deputy Canales to make haste with the
investigation. Without any eyewitnesses the
investigation was merely a formality.

Garcia's investigation began in earnest the
following day. The first order of business was to
view the body of the murder victim. Garcia called
on Ernest, the town mayor, magistrate, and
notary public at his general store off the main
street.

The deceased body was stored in a crude morgue with a corrugated tin roof, added to the back of the store. One small window faced east and was set high enough on the wall to keep curious youngsters from peering in on the dead.

Ernest, as magistrate, had pronounced the deceased dead of traumatic insult, since the rifle bullet which had entered the chest cavity of the victim from front-to-back, just above the wishbone. The bullet had exited the body and was lost somewhere in the wide-open, spacious front yard of Romo's estate. No one had bothered to look for the bullet. Now, more than a week later, it was a moot-point to even look. Not much could be learned from the bullet itself. It was a narrow caliber, possibly even a steel-bullet, since the entry and exit holes appeared to be exactly the same diameter. There was constant foot, horse, and wagon traffic where the victim had dropped from the fatal rifle shot. Deputy Canales jotted down some quick, pertinent facts for his official report: 1). Death by traumatic insult (as already determined by the presiding magistrate), a narrow caliber, most probably a rifle bullet. 2). The bullet itself was not recovered. 3). No eyewitnesses, no one saw from which direction the bullet had been fired.

Deputy-Investigator Adrian Canales finished his notes for his official report and removed himself with haste from the make-shift morgue.

He blanched and nearly puked from the overpowering stench of the murder victim's putrid corpse. He concluded his official investigation with a final note: Case Closed—No further investigation required. As he left Ernest's store, he proposed that the victim should be given a Christian burial as soon as possible. Tiny flies had already accumulated on and about the dead body. Then he rode back to the County Seat in San Diego, Texas to file his official report, relinquish his prestigious "investigator" title (until the next time), and to recommence his mundane duties as just another Deputy Sheriff.

Don Baltazar Romo continued professing his innocence even though no one was brave enough to suggest to his face that he might be complicit in his son-in-law's death. Life continued without Enrique Garcia. His widow eventually married another man who almost immediately relocated with her to San Antonio. And it seemed that the story of the mysterious death of Enrique Garcia would be forever forgotten.

One late, spring day a new cowboy was hired by the Romo Ranch. He knew horses and cattle, and he was young and strong and exulted confidence. The only thing that vaguely troubled old *Don* Baltazar was that this young cowboy's name was *Garcia*, however, that was a common enough

54

name. None-the-less, *Don* Baltazar asked this young cowboy if he knew a former ranch employee by the same last name, the late Enrique Garcia? The young cowboy simply met *Don* Baltazar's gaze and he shook his head in a negative gesture.

The new cowboy had been working for the Romo Ranch for less than a month when an early summer thunderstorm brewed up. Lightning flashed and thunder pealed, and large, heavy cold raindrops started coming down with a vengeance. It was as if the very heavens were aghast with the horrid deeds of some men.

Old *Don* Baltazar hurried upstairs to close the window, the very same open window he had shot Enrique Garcia through. As *Don* Baltazar raised his arms to shut the window, a flash of lightning struck at the window. *Don* Baltazar dropped dead on the floor of a lightning strike.

The ranch hands murmured that Baltazar had died of a lightning bolt that had come through the same open window he had fired the fatal rifle shot that killed Enrique Garcia. Divine providence?

"No," commented the new cowboy, "lightning did not kill the old man, I did. I shot him though the same open window that he fired through to kill my cousin." With that he slid his Winchester into his saddle scabbard, got on his horse and rode south.

Lechuza

Chapter 5

Pilfered Gold

During the first decade of this century, I hired on with a medium-size Texas horse and cattle ranch. The ranch was known as *El Rancho Escondido* (the Hidden Ranch). Perhaps in all, there were a half-dozen employees, most were old cowboys, cooks, and some part-time help.

Sammy, the ranch foreman, lived on the property in a house provided for his family by the ranch. Among the more interesting aspects of our duties were the finding of dead undocumented illegal immigrants on the property, all in all, some 20,000 acres. The ranch hands would usually be the first to find a dead person on the property. As ranch security, I would be notified first, and then I would notify the general manager, the foreman, the local authorities, and I would record the findings in report-form for the people who owned the ranch.

It was during this time that I coined this saying: "*On a good day, nothing happens. On a bad day, we find the mortal remains of some poor soul and we try to find enough physical evidence to give his loved ones' closure. And on a particularly good*

57

day, by the Grace of God, we manage to help save someone's life."

Sammy's job required that he live at the ranch itself. I lived in my own house, not far from the ranch headquarters, so I drove by Sammy's house every day. Sometimes, several times a day.

Since I lived within driving distance from Sammy's house, I often stopped by to converse with him about the usual lack of rain, the heat, or other matters pertaining to ranch operations. About once a month, Sammy and Delores would invite me to have dinner with them.

That hot, summer afternoon, Sammy and I sat in the front patio of his house waiting for Delores to ring the dinner bell. The patio faced east, and there always seemed to be a gentle breeze blowing out of the southeast. This made sitting in his patio, enjoying fresh sun-tea, wonderfully comfortable, even as the blistering hot sun set in the west.

There is only so much small talk one can make, concerning the rain or lack of rain. So, having depleted that topic, Sammy started telling me a story which occurred at this ranch some thirty years earlier, when he first started working for El Rancho Escondido.

Lechuza

"The original owner of Rancho Escondido," Sammy began, "was very wealthy." He paused to take a hard drag on his cigarette before continuing. "Do you have any idea how rich he was?"

"Not really Sammy. I never met the gentleman, and if he was as rich as you say, we probably didn't move in the same circles." I was trying for a little sarcastic humor but it either went over Sammy's head, or he chose to ignore it.

"Well sir, let me give you some idea of how wealthy he was. He used a solid gold block, you know, about the size of a modern concrete construction block, for a door stop."

I took a cool drink from my frosty glass of ice-cold sun tea as I tried to visualize a block of solid gold being used in the fashion described. The gold hunk was probably 1,000 troy ounces of 24 karat gold. This would be more than twice the size of a 400 troy ounce, standard London Good Delivery gold bar.

In Houston, I was once offered a brick-size lump of pure silver that was used as a door stop in a coin shop. The silver was displayed on top of the glass counter and I walked slowly around it for a better view. "Now, Todd," I asked the vendor, "Exactly what would I do with a brick-size chunk

Lechuza

of pure silver the size of a standard carpentry brick?"

Todd shrugged, "I don't know, you could use it for a door stop, or melt it into silver bullets, or just wait until the price of silver goes up and sell it for a profit. I only want $800 for it as is."

"The price of silver has been very slow lately." I made eye-contact with Todd when I added, "I don't believe in werewolves, even though I have seen my share of monsters. And, if I tell my wife I paid $800 for a door stop, she'll hit me on the head with it."

We did not come to terms on the silver brick, but I did buy a silver piece-of-eight from the seventeenth century. A piece-of-eight, or *ocho reales* (eight bits), is a Spanish silver coin which became the basis for our own US dollar, thus the saying, *eight-bits-a-dollar*. The Spanish coin came with documentation to prove that it came from the famous Spanish treasure ship, *Nuestra Señora de Atocha*, (which went down during a hurricane on September 6, 1622, near Key West, Florida.) This silver coin was later gold-plated and looked very impressive. Many years later, I gave that silver coin to a niece who really liked it even after I explained to her that it was not real gold. She bought a gold chain and a bezel for it, and as far as I know, she still wears it on special occasions.

Lechuza

"So, tell me Sammy, what happened to the gold? Did the owner take it with him when he sold his ranch to the current owner?"

Sammy held his cigarette in his left hand as he set his iced tea down on the coffee table, "No, the gold disappeared one day."

"Disappeared?" I nearly did a double-take. "Sammy, even thirty years ago, a chunk of gold that size must have been worth over a million dollars. How did it just disappear?"

"It went missing. Probably a burglary. We found the front door to the boss' house wide open and the gold block was gone."

As a retired police officer my interest was aroused, "What else was taken?"

"Nothing," was his abrupt reply, "only the gold was taken."

"The house was not ransacked?"

"No, only the gold was taken."

"I suppose your boss was very upset?"

"No," Sammy replied matter-of-factly, "he didn't even call the Sheriff's Office to have a report made."

Lechuza

Now, Delores called us in for dinner.

I have often wondered about the missing gold. Gold does not represent value. Gold is value. This is why the very wealthy have traditionally hoarded gold. This is probably why the owner possessed this considerable chunk of gold and why it was hidden in plain sight. This, however, does not explain why the owner was not upset about losing his gold.

I can think of several reasons. The number one reason could be that he simply moved the gold to a safer location without telling anyone about it. Or the gold might not have been as valuable as one might think. It could have been less than 24 karats pure. A couple of hundred years ago, India minted a tiny gold coin, about the diameter of a shirt button. It was approximately six karat gold. The logic behind the Indian one tenth ounce gold Fanam coin was so that even the poorest of the poor could possess a bit of gold. Although not commonly known, gold can be as little as 6, 8, or 10 karats. What is better known and more often used in jewelry is the 12, 14 or 18 karat gold. If the doorstop gold block were any less pure than 22 or 24 karats, it would be worth proportionately less than my estimated million-plus-dollars.

Another possibility is that the doorstop gold block could have been a Doré bar, which is a mixture of gold and silver, usually created at the mine site, and less valuable than pure gold. Or it could have been a gag bar, that is, not gold at all but gold-plated-silver, or even painted lead. Remember the silver coin I gave to my niece that was only gold plated and not worth anything over the spot price of silver? It could have been a Good Delivery silver bar which weigh between 750 and 1,000 troy ounces (1,000 troy ounces of pure silver would weigh approximately 68 US pounds). These bars are pure silver, and measure 12"x5"x3-1/4". Dimension wise, this bar would be smaller than the bar Sammy described, but after thirty years, one's memory can become distorted.

I personally favor the Doré bar explanation for the doorstop gold brick. This is because of another little-known fact. From 1933 until 1986 it was unlawful for US Citizens to possess pure 24 karat gold. The exception were dentists who by the very nature of their medical work need gold for filling teeth. The reason the US Government prohibited American citizens from possessing gold was out of fear that American gold would leave the country to be sold on the international gold market for a premium. At least, this is the official explanation.

Even during the no-gold era, a very wealthy person could possess one or more Doré bars and technically not be in violation of the 1933, possession of gold act.

Eventually, Sammy and Delores left the Rancho Escondido to venture into other venues. I also became discontented with my job there and after the hunting season closed, I resigned my employment with El Rancho Escondido.

The Lady in White

Hunting is still a big event at Rancho Escondido. Extra hands are hired to help with the game processing and cooking. During bird-hunting season, outriders, or spotters, (extra cowboys on horseback), are hired to help spot the coveys of quail.

Three of the part-timers requested permission to stay in the office building, just walking distance north of Sammy and Delores' old house. The office building had a nice, semi-screened patio and a bathroom with a shower stall, which made it an ideal temporary guest house. The cowboys brought in their sleeping bags, cots, hammocks, TV/DVD player combo, extra fans, a microwave oven, and a couple of compact refrigerators. They would stay in the old office building exactly... *One night.*

When the general manager asked them why they were no longer staying in the old office, they explained that it was simply better to drive home each evening and spend the night at home, in their own beds. Which was and is, a very plausible explanation. One never sleeps as comfortably as in his own home, in his own bed.

Some days later, questions arose as to who was staying in the foreman's old house. The answer was, "No one, yet. It is being prepped for the new Foreman."

"New Foreman?" Someone asked?

"Well," replied the general manager, "he hasn't been hired yet. We're still looking at applications."

Some more days later, the rumor began circulating among the hands that strange sounds were heard emanating from the vicinity of the old foreman's house late at night.

"What kind of sounds?" I asked.

"I don't know," someone replied, "like a woman moaning or crying in the night."

I gave this some thought before replying, "Well, we all know how far sound can travel on a still, cool night. During hunting season, we have some neighbors who stay at a hunting camp a couple of miles to the south of us. The prevailing wind blows out of the southeast here. Perhaps they play their TV a little too loudly."

Well, into the second week of hunting season, another cowboy asked if he could stay in the old office building. This new cowboy was a friend of mine, by the name of *Andy* Garza.

"Sure," replied the general manager. "The other out riders stayed there for a couple of nights, then decided they were more comfortable in their own homes, in their own beds."

"Just watch out for *La Llorona* (the wailing woman)," the other part-timers cautioned the new cowboy, jovially.

Andy Garza replied, "I'm not afraid of anything."

Andy stayed exactly... *One* night.

Fortunately, I enjoyed good rapport with Andy and one afternoon I asked him what had happened the one night he stayed in the old office.

"Nothing," he replied, perhaps a little too quickly, "My parents are getting older and I figured I should stay closer to town in case they need something."

Lechuza

Not entirely satisfied with his answer but not
wishing to pry, I nodded, indicating that I
understood and accepted his explanation.

He must have read the quizzing expression on my
face because the following day, during our lunch
break, he took me aside to explain the real reason
he decided not to sleep in the old office building
anymore.

"I had a lucid dream," he stated simply.

"Do you want to talk about it?"

"Yes," he replied, "I was sleeping in the screened
patio that night in my hammock when I heard the
electronic gate begin to open."

The main entry gate to the Escondido Ranch
features a modern, key-code gate control that
works off a solar panel and a battery.

"Oh heck, that crazy gate has been known to open
if you just look at it wrong—"

 "No," the cowboy gestured with his hands and
facial expressions, "It was a lucid dream. At least I
am quite sure that it was a lucid dream," he
sighed and continued, "let me finish telling you..."

I am a rather good listener, and so I let the cowboy
finish telling his story.

"When I heard the gate start to open, I looked at my watch. It was three in the morning. I wondered who could be coming in at that time, and so I looked outside without leaving my hammock. A woman was walking away from the keypad. She waited for the gate to open a bit more, and then she started walking straight toward the office building where I had been sleeping, in the screened patio. She walked deliberately, unhurried, with a grim determination that unnerved me."

I hated to interrupt, but I had to ask the cowboy if he could describe the woman.

He nodded saying, "She was about this tall," indicating with his right hand that she stood about five and a half feet tall.

"She was dressed in a long, white dress and she had long, straight brown hair that came down to her shoulders. She was fine-boned and slim, and there was a spectral appearance to her. It was almost as if her makeup had a sprinkling of glitter in it. I feigned sleep because she was walking straight toward the screened patio. There was no other way out and there was nowhere to hide."

"Didn't you have your .45 Colt revolver with you?"

"I'm new here and I don't know how the boss would feel about me having a firearm with me, so I

68

left it in my pickup. Besides, God forbid, I wouldn't want to accidentally shoot anyone."

I could only repeat his *God forbid* statement.

Andy continued, "She opened the screen door and stood at the threshold staring at me. She seemed surprised to see someone sleeping there. I am not sure how long she stood there staring at me, but I continued to pretend that I was asleep."

Finally convinced that I was asleep, she entered the screened patio and walked straight for the main office door to her left. She tried turning the doorknob but found that it was locked. Then she ran her right hand over the wall-paneling to the right of the office door as if she were looking for something."

I said nothing, but I knew what she was looking for.

"That hollow-core door is in bad shape. I am sure she could have just broken in, but she probably was afraid to make too much noise and wake me."

Frustrated, she turned and stared at me. She must have wondered if I was really asleep. She faced the office door again, and again she ran her right hand over the paneling to the right of the door in an ever-widening circle. What was she looking for?

Lechuza

I spoke not a word even though I knew exactly what she was looking for on the wall to the right of the office door.

"Now the *Woman in White* started walking slowly toward me. I pretended to be asleep as she hovered closer and closer to my face. I could feel her breath on my face and neck. Not fetid, not hot, and not cold. Just a perfectly normal, human breath that made my own breath catch in my throat. Then she placed her right hand over my heart. Her hand felt unnaturally warm and dry as she let it rest over my heart. Finally, after what seemed an eternity, she turned to leave."

Again, I interrupted the cowboy, "May I ask you a question?"

"Of course,"

"What did she do when she left the building?"

Without hesitating the cowboy said, "She walked straight to the keypad and keyed in the code to open the gate. Again, I heard the gate begin to open and she casually walked toward the opening gate. She turned left and walked toward the highway."

I just nodded at my friend, Andy Garza.

Lechuza

The following day, I had some telephone calls to make to some friends in Houston. They had more medical experience than I and could perhaps resolve one question I still had about the mysterious *Woman in White.*

"Good morning Cirilia," I said cheerfully to my friend. "You used to work in the Medical Center before you became a police officer?"

"I did," Cirilia Salas answered cheerfully, obviously pleased to hear from me again.

"What would make a woman's hand feel unnaturally warm and dry to the touch? Severe diabetes?" I knew for fact that my number one suspect for the chimera disguised as the Woman in White, was severely diabetic.

"Not diabetes," Cirilia replied immediately, and she followed up with her own question, "What is her age?"

"I'm only guessing, but probably close to her mid, or late-forties?"

"The onset of menopause could do that."

"Thanks, Cirilia, you are the best."

Lechuza

There was no need to get a second opinion. I now know for certain who our mystery Woman in White was, and who she was not. The only thing I did not know and could only speculate about, was the reason for the charade. She was not a lucid dream and she was not a chimera.

The Woman in White was looking for something hidden in the old office. However, she could not know that I had removed the key that she was looking for. The door key that hung from a finishing nail in the panel to the right of the office door. The very key that would have opened the office door for her. I even removed the finishing nail to discourage anyone from simply hanging another key there.

"Keeping a key to the office on the outside wall may be convenient, but it is *not* good security," I said to the general manager as I handed him the office key. You keep this, and if you wish, make a copy for me."

As he struggled adding the key to the large keyring on his belt he commented, "That won't be necessary. In a few more weeks we'll be razing the old office to build a modern one in its place."

So, what was the Woman in White doing wandering around during the dead-of-night, trying to break into the Rancho Escondido Office? Obviously, she was looking for something of great value. What could possibly be more valuable than a London Good Delivery gold bar? I know Sammy described a larger gold bar, but memory can be a tricky thing. After all that time, Sammy must have embellished the size of the gold ingot in his mind. Gold ingots are made to a standard size and weight. This is so that they can be managed and moved around by one person. Anything larger than a 400 troy ounce, Good Delivery gold bar would be too heavy and unwieldy for a single person.

However, how could the *Woman in White* know that the gold bar was even there? Very easily, if she were an accomplice, along with her husband, to the original pilfering of the missing gold.

Why didn't they try to sell the gold years before? They probably did not realize how hard it is to sell pure gold on the black market, especially during an era when mere possession of pure, 24 karat gold, is unlawful. That law was rescinded in 1986, making it easier for individuals to possess and sell gold.

So how much could they expect to get for the gold bar? Well, the amount changes from day-to-day, and sometimes from hour-to-hour. Pure gold sells by the troy ounce. On a good day, $500,000 would not be impossible. Guessing that they lacked the right contacts to get the maximum dollars for their gold, any amount over $100,000 or $150,000

73

cash, would probably be acceptable. Or they could cut the gold bar into smaller pieces and sell what they needed to keep them in spending cash.

Why hide the gold in the office? If the gold were found in the office, they could just act surprised and ask, "Now how did that gold get there?"

But if the gold were found where they lived, (remember, it was not their house; the house they lived in belonged to the ranch), how could they explain the presence of the lost gold in their possession? That would be a very awkward situation.

Why did the Woman in White dress up like the most legendary apparition in Mexican history, *La Llorona*, the weeping or wailing woman? Superstition runs deep in south Texas. Anyone who should chance to see her, would be telling the story repeatedly to his children and grandchildren, about how he barely escaped with his life after coming face-to-face with *La Llorona*.

What finally became of the *Woman in White* and her husband?

Rumors in town tell about how they moved north and came into some money. Some people say they moved to San Antonio. Others say it was Austin. Still others say they had hit it big playing the Texas Lottery. Others say it was an inheritance.

Lechuza

Delores was even seen driving a brand-new, red Mercedes Benz, and Sammy a new, loaded Silverado truck.

What is the truth? I only know that the Statute of Limitations on the burglary and theft of the gold have long run out if they even pilfered the missing gold.

Remember also, the original owner did not even file a report with the local authorities. Was this because when the gold disappeared, it was unlawful to possess pure gold? Or was it because it was only a gag-bar, and not real gold at all? Or was it because he was so rich that he did not need the gold? In any case, no crime was reported, therefore, no crime was committed.

Since the law concerning possession of pure gold was rescinded, any US Citizen can possess as much pure gold as he can find. Did Sammy and Delores commit the perfect crime? *That* is not for me to say.

Lechuza

ψ

Chapter 6

Diana and the Demonic Cat

My family was still living in Houston, Texas. At the time, only our youngest daughter remained at home. It was a Friday night, and my wife Linda and I were lying in bed watching television. It was just after 10:00 pm, and we were expecting our daughter, Diana, to come in at any time.

Just then my cellphone rang. The ID said it was Diana, and I answered thinking that she was calling to notify us that she would be staying overnight at her friend's house.

"*Dad,*" my daughter yelled in a frantic tone, "*There's a demonic cat in the driveway. It is positively demonic.* I am afraid to get out of my car."

"Okay, Mi'ja," I told her, I'll be right out."

"What's Diana saying," my wife, who could plainly hear our daughter's frantic voice, asked?

"She is saying that there is a demonic cat in our driveway, and she is afraid to get out of her car."

As I started to walk outside my wife stopped me, "Wait," she exclaimed, "Aren't you going to take a gun?"

Lechuza

"What for," I replied, "If it is a cat, I won't need a gun. And if its demonic, a gun won't help."

"Oh," my wife replied, plainly grasping the truth of my logic.

All our children are animal lovers, and for quite some time we had been leaving cat food and water in two dishes outside on our front porch. Several stray cats canvased the neighborhood for food and my girls fancied that the stray cats were really theirs, and they diligently provided cat food for them.

One evening, while I was setting cat food out for the strays, a lady in a brand-new, white Jaguar parked by our driveway. She got down, opened the rear passenger door, and retrieved a twenty-pound bag of cat food. Smiling, she handed the cat food to me, saying, "I see you're a cat lover, too."

I nodded and thanked the kind lady for the cat food, all the while thinking, *God bless the beasts and kind strangers.*

One of the cats, an orange female we fondly called *Clipped Ear kitten,* was really friendly and if we had not owned a long-hair Apple-head Chihuahua female, and a white miniature French Poodle, we would have probably taken this orange feline in. Her ear was clipped, indicating that some humane society had already fixed and vaccinated her and released her. Clipped Ear was the real reason we left food and water out, but never imagined the cat food would attract a *demonic cat.*

As I stepped out onto our front step, I could see my daughter cowering behind the steering wheel of her car. A very real fear was visible on her pretty face.

She cracked her driver's side window and yelled out, "There it is Dad, it's positively demonic!"

Munching away at the cat food I saw an old, gray opossum, possibly nearly twice the size of the stray cats, its back appeared deformed as it dipped its head into the food bowl. Its long tail was devoid of hair making it an eerie pink in color. His face was a mask of fine, white hair, which added to his bizarre appearance. In the headlights of Diana's car, the opossum's eyes seemed huge, and glowed an eerie yellow orange. Opossum's eyes can completely dilate for superior night-vison. This made this opossum's eyes truly seem demonic.

"Diana," I yelled out, trying to sound reassuring, "it's not a cat, Mi'ja, it's just an old opossum."

Lechuza

The opossum was ravenous, oblivious to everything except the now nearly empty dish of cat food. I was a bit puzzled that this old opossum was not just eating what opossums usually eat, crickets, insects, small snakes, snails, slugs, and spiders. In the United States we tend to use the word *possum* synonymously with *opossum*. The opossum is the only marsupial mammal indigenous to North America. Like their cousins, the true possums, native to Australia and New Guinea, they are marsupial, mostly nocturnal, and arboreal.

I stomped my right foot down hard on the concrete driveway and yelled, "Shoo!" The opossum totally ignored me, which kind of offended me. The old opossum was making me look weak in front of my youngest daughter and so, I boldly stomped toward the opossum. "Shoo!" I shouted again. Again, I was ignored.

Now I clapped hard at the big, rodent-like creature, barely connecting with the end of his left ear. Now I had his attention. It hurriedly scurried away running into everything in sight. It hugged the garage wall as it fled. *OMG*, I thought, *I scared a blind opossum!*

"Alright Diana," I assured my daughter, "it was just an old opossum.

Lechuza

Without a word my daughter hurried inside. I could hear Diana excitedly telling her mother about the demonic cat.

I found an old, cracked dish and I filled it with cat food. I went back outside and set the cat food down out of sight from our driveway.

The old opossum was scurrying along the wall of our garage and our privacy fence still trying to escape from the ogre who had scared him.

The opossum had found the cat food, by smell no doubt, and was happily munching away when I brought him a bowl of water. The poor, old guy barely sensed my presence.

They are immune to the bite of the deadly rattlesnake and other venomous snakes, other than the Coral snake, which they can usually kill and eat before being snake bitten. Some people make pets of them even though most people consider them ugly, as they do resemble, somewhat, a large rat. I think that they are interesting mammals.

I never told Diana, but I continued feeding her demonic cat for several weeks. I learned that he really liked a certain brand of cat food which was very aromatic, and so I kept a good supply for both the stray cats and the demonic cat.

Lechuza

Occasionally, I left sardines or some left-over tuna or salmon for him to eat.

One day he stopped coming. I knew that he was an older opossum and I figured that his time had come. I fancy that I made his last few weeks better, and I hope that he eventually forgave me for scaring him so badly. That was not one of my finest moments.

Chapter 7

The Dark Night of The Mannequin
(The Legend of Pascualita)

In the modern-day city of Chihuahua, (State
Capital of Chihuahua,) in Northern Mexico, there
is a bridal shop named, *La Popular—La Casa de
Pascualita*. The original owner of this shop was
Pascuala Esparza-Perales de Pérez.

Pascuala had a beautiful young daughter called
Pascualita. Today, nobody can remember
Pascualita's real name, and so she shall forever be
remembered only as *Pascualita*.

According to the legend, Pascuala Esparza
dreamed of the day that she could see her
beautiful Pascualita dressed up as a bride, in an
exquisite custom-made white wedding dress. And
so, it seemed that Pascuala's dream would finally
be realized, for in 1930, Pascualita met her soon-
to-be-bridegroom. The date for their wedding was
set, however, fate cruelly devised other plans for
Pascualita.

Pascualita died on her wedding day in front of the
altar, the victim of a deadly arachnid. Some say
that it was a lethal scorpion hiding in her tiara

that stung Pascualita. Others say that it was the bite of a brown recluse spider. Still others tell that it was a jealous black widow spider that caused Pascualita's untimely death.

In all fairness to black widow spiders, according to arachnologists, the idea that the female black widow spider kills her mate shortly after mating is erroneous. Although it may occasionally happen. When it does, it appears to be accidental rather than intentional. The female spider is the larger of the species and its venom is deadlier, drop for drop, than the venom of the dreaded Western Diamondback rattlesnake.

Be that as it may, Pascualita died on her wedding day. Whatever became of Pascualita's grieving betrothed is not even mentioned, nor is his name remembered, as is often the case in old tales.

Pascuala Esparza could not bear the thought of never seeing her beautiful daughter dressed up in her bridal gown. So rather than have Pascualita interned in the family crypt, she took her daughter's lifeless body to a master taxidermist to be preserved for all time.

On March 25, 1930, a new mannequin was installed in *La Popular* storefront window. This mannequin was beautiful, life-like, tall, and svelte. Her wide-set glass eyes seemed to follow you around. Her hair and skin tone were all too real.

Moreover, her hands were entirely too life-like. Before long, someone commented that the mannequin bore an uncanny resemblance to the store owner.

"No, wait," someone else remarked, *"She looks exactly like Pascualita, Pascuala's daughter!"*

Wrong or right, people concluded that this mannequin was not a mannequin at all, but the embalmed body of Pascuala Esparza's recently deceased daughter. The very one who had recently died on her wedding day of some type of spider bite.

The town's people began to express their disapproval, but the story took on a life of its own. By the time Pascuala prepared an official statement declaring that the allegations were not true, nobody was willing to believe her. The legend of La Pascualita was born.

People began to claim that Pascualita changed positions of her own volition during the night in the storefront window, even though the store was closed and locked, and no one was around to adjust her stance. It was also said that her facial expression changed as you glanced her way.

Only two employees can change Pascualita's wedding dress behind the closed curtains of La Popular storefront window. Her dress is changed

twice a week. Those employees charged with
changing Pascualita's dress say that her hands
are very life-like. Pores, fine hair, and even
fingerprints can be discerned on her hands.

One of the two employees also tell that she has
seen perspiration on her hands. They also state
that Pascualita is so life-like, that she has varicose
veins on her legs. Can any taxidermist (or
mannequin-maker, as the case may be), be so
skilled at his art that he can include such details?

It is also rumored that Pascualita's hair has begun
to gray and continues to grow. Her fingernails
must be trimmed as they also continue to grow.

People begin coming from all over Mexico to see
Pascualita in the storefront window. Many women
would buy the wedding dress that Pascualita was
wearing on the day they visited *La Popular.* A
superstition was born. It was said that this would
ensure a long and happy marriage for the woman
fortunate enough to buy the wedding dress that
Pascualita was modeling on the day of their visit.

As the stories spread, people started coming to La
Popular from all over South America. Then people
started coming from the United States, Canada,
and even Europe.

One young lady stated that her ex-boyfriend was
chasing her with a gun in hand, intent on killing

her. *Si no mia, de nadien,* (if you will not be mine, nobody can have you.) The terrified young lady ran across the street hoping to elude her ex-boyfriend.

As he fired his gun, she looked up and saw Pascualita in the storefront window. *Save me, Pascualita,* she pleaded, and fell unconscious at the storefront. She was transported to the hospital where she recovered from the non-fatal gunshot to her back.

She insisted that Pascualita was a saint who had saved her life, and when she left the hospital, she started taking votive candles to La Popular. Indeed, many of the local people came to consider Pascualita a folk-saint, (that is, someone considered a saint by the public in general, but not canonized by the Roman Catholic Church). The young lady who owed her life to Pascualita was asked to take the candles to the Basilica, as it became impossible to accommodate so many candles at the La Popular store.

The legend of Pascualita also states that one day, a French master magician came to the City of Chihuahua. It is not certain if he came to Chihuahua expressly to see Pascualita, or if he just happened to be in the city. His name was *Henri Pierre Héron,* and he performed under the stage name, *Henri Étonnant,* which translates into the *Astounding Henri. The Astounding Henri,*

however, was not in Chihuahua to perform. He
was on a Sabbatical. Be that as it may, many
came to believe that Henri gave the most
astounding performance of his career in the City
of Chihuahua before an audience of one.

Shortly after arriving in Chihuahua, Henri
gravitated to *La Popular* in the center of the city.
He immediately became entranced with the
beautiful Pascualita in the storefront window of La
Popular. Witnesses stated that at night, Henri
Héron and Pascualita could be seen dancing
together inside the closed bridal shop. Many said
the two were seen walking arm-in-arm, late at
night, in the town plaza and even along the nearby
lake shore.

Did Henri use dark magic to bring Pascualita to
life? Those who believe that Henri used the
forbidden art of *necromancy* to bring Pascualita to
life also tell that the Lord sent one of His
Archangels to confront master magician Henri
Héron.

For his transgression, Henri Pierre Héron was
ordered to leave Mexico and to board the
Vliegende Hollander, the legendary Dutch ghost
ship that can never make port and is doomed to
sail the Seven Seas forever. Whatever misgivings
Henri may have had when the Archangel
confronted him dissipated like smoke when the
Archangel said to him, "I am an envoy of the Lord,

88

Lechuza

Henri, *C'est Dieu qui te commande* (It is God Who Commands you)."

Consequently, Henri made his way to Guaymas, the nearest seaport, some 298 miles west of Chihuahua. He drove nonstop for ten hours. Once there, Henri purchased a ten-foot rowboat from a local fisherman, paying for the rowboat with a twenty-peso gold coin. Money was no longer of any consequence to Henri. He rowed out to rendezvous with the *Vliegende Hollander* that awaited Henri in the open sea. As Henri boarded the *Vliegende Hollander*, witnesses from the shore stated that a terrible storm could be seen brewing in the west, which apparently came out of nowhere.

As the ship sailed away, the storm followed the ship in its wake. Henri Héron was never heard of or seen again. Small wonder. Vliegende Hollander is *Dutch* for *The Flying Dutchman*.

Can Pascualita still be seen in the storefront window of La Popular Bridal Shop?

Some say with all the conviction of one who is certain of the facts, that Pascualita still resides at Calle 803, 31000 Chihuahua, Chihuahua. La Popular Bridal Shop, is, after all, *La Casa De Pascualita*.

So, if you're ever in the City of Chihuahua be sure to look her up. Just do not stare into her clear brown eyes for too long, lest you come under her spell as Henri Pierre Héron did.

If you are a bride-to-be, consider purchasing the wedding dress that Pascualita is modeling on the day of your visit to La Popular. After all, the Legend of La Pascualita guarantees that brides who do marry in the gown Pascualita is wearing on the day of their visit will be blessed with a happy marriage.

Chapter 8

A Night for Fireflies

During 2008, until 2010, I operated a small, bird-hunting camp in South Texas. When White Wing dove season opened in early fall, I would become extremely busy.

The entire camp was less than fifty acres, but it was ideally located in the middle of nowhere, away from heavy traffic and prying eyes. My primary duties were keeping accurate records for the game warden. This included making sure that each hunter had the proper hunting license and a legal shotgun. The magazine capacity had to be limited to two shells, plus one in the chamber. Camp-rules limited the gauge of the shotgun to be 20, or 12 gauge, although at my discretion I could allow a hunter to shoot a legal, 10-gauge shotgun.

One hunter liked to shoot an old, black-powder, 10-gauge double-barrel. I was shocked by how loud this old 10-gauge was, but if the other hunters did not complain, I was willing to let him use this behemoth old shotgun that once belonged to his grandfather. No one ever complained. It seemed that all the hunters used hearing protection as required by the camp rules.

Lechuza

The camp featured a man-made pond, approximately one-and-a-half acres in diameter and approximately fifteen feet deep. The pond attracted the White Wing Doves and the hunters concealed themselves in the surrounding native mesquite brush, or in camouflaged pop-up blinds sold expressly for this purpose. The freshwater pond was stocked with Channel and Blue Catfish, Copper-nose Bluegill, and Large Mouth Bass. The hunters frequently told me that they were surprised that every time they shot a dove that landed in the water, a big catfish would immediately swallow it. Blue Catfish are the largest freshwater catfish in North America. Examples of Blue Catfish exceeding a hundred pounds in weight are not unheard of. I once caught a Blue Catfish in this pond that was longer than my leg from hip to ankle. I estimated the weight to be twenty-plus pounds. It was just a catch-and-release, because it was more fish than one person could consume in one meal.

There were also two cabins, that is, one small cabin (for my use), and a bigger cabin, or bunkhouse, for the hunters who wished to spend the weekend. The bunkhouse featured three bathrooms, a common area for preparing meals, watching TV, fraternizing, and sleeping. The bunkhouse could accommodate up to a maximum of a dozen adults, in built-along-the-wall bunk beds, cots, air mattresses, or sleeping bags.

However, eight occupants or less were considered full capacity. The bunkhouse also featured a small bedroom with a bathroom at the far north end of the bunkhouse. This was in case one of the hunters should bring his wife and they desired a little more privacy.

The smaller cabin featured a screened back patio that one year was used by an overflow of four hunters who chose to spend the night in there, sleeping on their own cots. They preferred staying there for one night, rather than in the crowded bunk house, or driving into town to stay in a motel. No one ever complained, and everyone seemed to have fun.

It was during the second White Wing Dove hunting season that I first encountered the fireflies. I had not seen so many fireflies since I was a teenager growing up in Hebbronville, Texas. My mom and dad's house was located by a creek and some nights the fireflies lit up the entire vacant lot between the house and the creek. Some nights I would just walk over to that vacant lot to see the fireflies closeup.

If I stood still long enough, they would light on my arms, shirt, and hair. I tried never to hurt them as I perceived them as beautiful, benign insects. I did now and then, entertain the notion of filling a mason jar with fireflies to see if I could use the filled jar as a lantern. I never did though, for fear of injuring the fireflies.

Many, many years later, I was in Ashville, North Carolina for a wedding with my wife and one of her sisters. Around 10:00 pm, my sister-in-law accosted me and insisted that I accompany her.

"Where?" I asked.

"It's not too far and it is a place I've always wanted to visit, but I don't want to go alone. We'll be back before anyone misses us."

We walked out to our rented SUV and drove up a winding mountain road guided by her pre-programed GPS device. "It's a place known as *lover's leap*," Alma, my sister-in-law, stated. "Two lovers who couldn't be together because of parental disapproval," Alma continued, "came up here one night, and hand-in-hand, they both jumped off this mountain. They fell some three-thousand feet to their death."

"Ever since I read about this in High School, I have been intrigued by the story and I have wanted to see this place for myself." Alma wrapped the story up as we found the parking area to Lover's Leap.

Fortunately, no one else was around, as there appeared to only be parking for two cars.

Lechuza

The outcropping of rock at the mountain peak was encircled by a sturdy, chain link fence.

"This must be the place from where they leapt," I said to Alma as we both walked right up to the chain link fence. The sight was breathtaking. I looked up and I looked down and it was difficult to distinguish between up and down.

Above us, the white clouds sailed by and the star-filled sky appeared full of fireflies. Below us, mist drifting on the gentle breeze appeared as smaller clouds. And the fireflies below us appeared as stars twinkling and dancing carelessly among the clouds of mist. We both wished we had a camera, but we realized that the sight was far too panoramic to capture with a simple camera. When this happened, cellular phones had yet to come equipped with cameras.

We both sighed and sat on the bench conveniently provided for us in the viewing area. I do not think we spoke a single word while we sat on that bench so close to Heaven and so far above the fireflies. This must have been what the two lovers experienced as they fell to their deaths.

After about a half-an-hour, we looked at each other and wordlessly realized that it was time to leave this mountain and rejoin the wedding party in Ashville.

We drove back in silence. I think I finally managed to tell my sister-in-law, "Thank you for bringing me to such a beautiful place."

"The lovers," Alma mentioned, "I have often wondered if they were—"

"Forgiven? I interrupted, "Forgiveness is in God's Providence. Only He can decide, and His decisions are final."

Back in Ashville, only my oldest daughter, Marissa, asked me where I had disappeared to for nearly an hour. "Your aunt wanted to see Lover's Leap, and she didn't want to go alone." My daughter nodded; perhaps Alma had already shared with her that she wanted to see Lover's Leap.

During the second White Wing season, I hurried back to the hunting camp just after dark, from nearby Hebbronville town. The first of the hunters would start arriving within two hours and I had to fire up the 29-gallon, propane water heater.

I parked my pickup truck by the north-side entry door to my cabin, and I walked toward the bunkhouse to fire up the water heater. Walking in the dark toward the bunkhouse I was startled by the number of fireflies in the clearing between the bunkhouse and the cabin.

It was overcast, and the rumble of thunder was in the air. Sudden flashes of lightning illuminated the midnight-blue night sky. Beneath the low-hanging canopy of thunderhead clouds came big, cold, wet drops of rain intermittently spaced. The rain did not seem to bother the fireflies which continued to dart every which way. Up, down, side-ways. I should have been fearful of a lightning strike, but the beauty of the night and the splendorous display of fireflies, gave me a false sense of security.

None-the-less, I had to hurry and fire up the water heater. This involved manually opening three valves which led from the propane tank 150 feet west of the bunkhouse. I opened the first two valves located by the propane fuel tank itself, and then I jogged toward the last valve by the water heater in the water closet against the west wall of the bunkhouse. Just then, something in the sky caught my eye making me stop in midstride.

A meteor? No, a meteor would have to penetrate the low cloud canopy and then it would have only three to five-hundred yards to fall before impacting with the Earth. This was not a meteor. Meteors do not dally, scurrying from thunderhead to thunderhead, before falling directly and rapidly to the Earth. This strange orb of light seemed to be the size of a standard baseball, perfectly round and darting from thunderhead to thunderhead, blinking on and off and mimicking the actions of the fireflies.

I stared at the strange sight for two or three minutes. Should I run to the other cabin and grab my 8x32 binoculars to better observe this odd light? It did not seem to be going anywhere and so I decided to first fire up the propane water heater and then I could observe the odd orb of light to my heart's content.

Of course, the water heater decided to become obstinate and it took me longer than usual to fire it up. By the time I grabbed my binoculars, the orb of light in the sky was nowhere to be seen.

I retrieved my binoculars just the same, and I scanned the sky for the orb of light. Nothing but flashes of lightning and the big, fat raindrops that plopped on the lenses of my binoculars every time I looked up, blurring my vision.

Soon the hunters started to arrive, and I became busy recording their information and hunting license numbers on the camp ledger. Then I would escort them one by one to the bunkhouse. John, one of the hunters, commented, "I have never seen so many fireflies in my entire life."

"I have John, but it was on a mountain in North Carolina." Fearing that John would think I was crazy, I never mentioned the large orb I had seen dancing between the thunderheads.

A few years later, while sitting on the tailgate of my friend Tom's truck with his wife Cirilia, we admired the big, South Texas night sky, I thought to share this story with my friends.

Tim commented, "Sounds like you witnessed a phenomenon few have ever seen. It is known as *ball lightning*."

Cirilia, sitting comfortably between the two of us, chimed in, "Ball lightning?"

"Yes," Tim answered, "Scientists cannot agree if it even exists, but there are stories. It's not like regular lightning but it does appear during thunderstorms, so people started calling it ball lightning."

"What is it?" Cirilia asked.

"Scientists think that if it does exist, it must be a clump of plasma." Tim cleared his throat and continued, "You see, witnesses also claim that ball lightning has the ability to pass through glass windows and even solid walls without damaging them."

"And here I was thinking that it was either a jumbo firefly or," I added, "at least a cluster of fireflies in a mating ritual."

Tom smiled saying, "I don't think fireflies can fly that high."

I had to agree with my friend.

✹

Chapter 9

Dybbuk

Do ghosts and spirits become attached to houses, places, animals or persons? According to certain Jewish folklore, spirits can also become attached to objects. In Yiddish, such a spirit, or the object to which it becomes attached, is known as a *dybbuk* (a malicious, clinging spirit).

Dybbuk boxes are now sold online usually to the highest bidder. They are typically old wine boxes from the time of the Holocaust. But the sale comes with the stipulation that the wine box must never be opened since dire consequences could result should this proviso be ignored. This warning is so grave, that at times, some of these boxes are sealed with wax. This, however, is not always the case.

My youngest brother, Eusebio, has lived in the Monterrey, Nuevo Leon (Mexico), most of his adult life. He married a young lady from the area named Laura Garza and were blessed with three beautiful girls. They remained married until Laura passed away after a long illness.

Chevo, as we called Eusebio, had a house built in
Monterrey. As their family grew, they decided to
add a second floor to their home. They converted
this new second floor into the bedroom area of
their home, and the first floor became the living
area. Their three daughters, Laurita, Diana, and
Rosio were either in college, or college graduates
by the time of their mother's passing.

When the girls were young, Laura's mother had an
armoire in her house that her daughter always
admired. Laurita's grandmother told her that she
could have the old armoire, which had been a gift
from her late, second husband, Mario Peña-Tovar,
(no relation to Laurita and her sisters). The
armoire was soon moved into the second floor of
the home Laurita shared with her sisters and their
father. The armoire was some six feet high, and
approximately four feet wide. It was made of a
medium-blonde wood, had two large
compartments to hang clothes on either side, and
a series of five drawers in the middle. It is believed
that the armoire had been constructed in Mexico,
sometime during the late 1800's or early 1900's.
During this era, houses usually did not have
built-in closets. Armoires served as closets do
today.

Not too many weeks after the armoire was brought
into their home, a life-long friend of the family

arrived. She was invited to stay with the family until she found her own apartment closer to the University. This friend, Dulce Zelaya, originally from Honduras, became the first witness to the bizarre and unsettling series of events which were soon to follow.

Dulce and her husband Larry were sleeping in one of the upstairs bedrooms. Dulce decided to use the bathroom at the end of the hall. Next to the bathroom door was a brown easy chair that shared the same corridor as the armoire.

Dulce was practically a family member to the Hinojosa Family, so imagine her surprise as she walked toward the bathroom, to see a stranger sitting in the brown easy chair just to the right of the bathroom door. This woman was not only a stranger, she was out of time and out of place, attired in a long dress with black, lace-up riding boots. The surrealism of the circumstance frightened Dulce so much that she turned around and ran to her bedroom.

Quickly she roused her husband and explained the situation. Larry did not waste any time getting up to investigate, but by the time he got to the easy chair, there was no one around. No one was in the corridor and no one was in the bathroom. It did not occur to Larry or Dulce to see if anyone was hiding in the armoire. Perhaps not wishing to offend their hosts, Dulce and Larry did not immediately share the events of that night with their friends.

When they did eventually talk about it, Chevo did recall that he had on occasion heard what could have been footsteps coming from the upstairs when he was alone in the house. These sounds were to be expected. The upper floor was not even two years old and Chevo attributed the odd sounds to the house settling. Laurita did remember seeing a reflection for a fleeting moment, of a strange woman wearing an old-fashioned woman's hat in the bathroom mirror. She quickly turned around and no one was there. Was this a quirk of the light, or her imagination? Even though she dismissed the incident nearly immediately, it appears that Laurita, (owner of the armoire) was the second witness.

After Chevo's wife, Laura, passed away, the traditional Novenas followed. Novenas are a series of nine consecutive devotional prayers, (or the praying of the Rosary), during nine consecutive days, for the eternal rest of the deceased person.

The prayers began at 7:00 p.m., to allow the people time to arrive at the Church from work. Rosío, the youngest daughter, had to drive the farthest, and missed most of the Novenas.

Rather than arrive late to Church, Rosío let herself in their house and waited for her father and sisters to return from Church. That day, Rosío became the third witness.

As she entered the home as she had done countless of times in the past, she was surprised to see that the family puppy, a white swiss shepherd, was behaving strangely. He stood like a sentinel at the foot of the stairs, one paw on the first step, looking up and barking and growling fiercely at something at the top of the stairs which Rosío could not see. The fearless pup was not going to let whatever it was come down the stairs, but neither would he allow Rosío to go up. When she tried, the pup turned sideways blocking her way with his body, and whimpering piteously as if to say, *do not go up the stairs, it is not safe up there!*

This was strange behavior indeed for the normally friendly, playful, and lovable puppy. Rosío decided to heed the pup's unseemly behavior and instead drove to the Church to rendezvous with her Dad and sisters.

The prayers were about to end when she located her father and sisters. As they left the Church and walked toward their cars, Rosío apprised her family of the incident with the family pup. They all hurried home from the Church and were pleased to see that the puppy was back to his normal self.

Lechuza

Some two weeks after the incident, Laurita was in the upstairs bathroom when again she saw the reflection in the mirror of the woman wearing the old-fashioned hat. When Laurita turned around, the woman was standing behind her.

Very frightened, Laurita ran downstairs to get her father. *"There is a strange woman in the upstairs bathroom Dad,"* Laurita exclaimed.

Chevo proceeded up the stairs determined to solve the mystery of the strange woman once and for all. The only other person in the house was Rosío, and by this time of night she was already asleep.

As he approached the bathroom, he could see that the door was ajar, and that the bathroom lights were on. Chevo started to open the bathroom door. Suddenly, the bathroom door was closed with such force that he was literally pushed away from the door. *Oh,* Chevo reasoned, *Rosío must be using the bathroom. Mystery solved!* And he turned to tell his daughter Laurita that it was her sister Rosío who was using the bathroom. Chevo was astonished to realize that Rosío was *not* in the bathroom, Rosío was the person standing behind him, not Laurita.

After that last occurrence, Laurita and her father decided to get rid of the armoire. A son of the original owner lived in town. Ignacio 'Nacho' Peña, son of Mario Peña-Tovar, was contacted. He remembered the armoire and stated that he was a carpenter by trade, and he had once done some repair work on it. He agreed to come for the armoire.

Two years later, Ignacio contacted Chevo to inform him that since taking the armoire home, they experienced anomalous events almost daily. He and his brother finally took the armoire outside and chopped it to pieces with an axe and burned all the pieces. The disturbances ceased.

Lechuza

Chapter 10

Restless Spirits

In 2008, Henri Garza purchased a house where a 46-year-old female, Socorro Barrera, was stabbed to death. In fact, several tragedies occurred, during the time that the original owners lived in this house. Socorro's husband, Juan Barrera, died in a horrific automobile crash while fleeing from unknown persons. He was killed near the house he shared with his wife and children when he lost control of his car on US Hwy 281. His car rolled several times before striking a palm tree. His body remained seat-belted within the car. Juan's severed head rolled and was finally found several yards from where his car came to rest.

Hernán, the author, diligently took notes as Henri continued with her story:

Socorro was attacked in her sleep by a knife-wielding attacker. She managed to crawl from the master bedroom into the bedroom just across the hallway, where she perished of blood loss and trauma. Her head was nearly severed from her body during the attack. The authorities later determined that the murderer was her own brother-in-law.

109

"As if this were not bad enough, Georgie Barrera, the older of their two sons, was murdered in Mexico. Perhaps Georgie was at the wrong place at the wrong time. Or perhaps Georgie was the victim of a drug deal that went wrong. The persons responsible for Georgie's death attempted to dispose of his body by burning it in a 55-gallon steel drum. They were unsuccessful."

"I'm not surprised Henri," Hernán interjected. "Impromptu cremations are largely unsuccessful, except in the movies. The average adult human body is approximately between fifty and seventy percent water. This high-water content makes disposing of a body by burning exceedingly difficult unless you have access to a crematorium."

Henri continued, "Whatever led to the circumstances surrounding the appalling deaths of the Barreras, the fact remains that at least three ghosts roam the house I have called home since 2008. The realtor did disclose the grisly details of the untimely deaths of the former owners before we closed the sale."

So, you may wonder why Henri decided to purchase the house anyway? The answer is quite simple, the price was right for a working, divorced mother of three children.

"So now you are privy to the condensed version of *Henri's House of Horrors*. On a similar note, many friends have asked me if I have tried to cleanse the house of the haunting ghosts?" Henri said. "Indeed, I have. Just after moving in, I tried blessing the house with a white candle intended for cleansing the house of unwanted spirits. No sooner had I lit the candle and walked away than it exploded into many pieces. It sounded as if all the windows in the house had shattered at once. I was almost relieved when I learned that it was the candle which had shattered, rather than the windows."

Once they moved into their new home, Jorge, Henri's oldest, settled into the master bedroom. This was Socorro's old bedroom. In the morning, Henri's son said, "Look Mom," and he raised the back of his T-shirt to show her his back.

There were numerous bright, red scratches all over his back as if someone with long fingernails had scratched him.

Alarmed Henri asked him, "Who did this to you, son?"

Jorge replied, "Socorro," He did not have to elaborate. We both knew who he was speaking of. Socorro Barrera, the former owner of our home.

Lechuza

That same day they changed bedrooms. Jorge moved into one of the other bedrooms and Henri moved into the master bedroom.

Henri added, "I have what has been described as long, silky raven hair, and so I wear my hair shoulder-length. I try to keep my black hair looking pretty and apparently it has attracted the attention of someone from the other realm. Often, while I am napping or sleeping, someone will pull on my hair with enough force to wake me up. When I look, no one is around."

When Henri's children grew up and left the house, Henri stored their toys in the attic. Then she started noticing that around midnight, the upstairs lights would turn on by themselves. The toys started acting as if someone were playing with them. A toy fire engine with a siren that sounds when someone manually rolls it on the floor would sound, as if a child's hand were playing with it, rolling it on the floor. Children could be heard giggling as they played with the toys.

Downstairs in the kitchen, Henri found a large ice cream carton on the floor, the freezer door was left open. Nothing was spilled. It was as if someone had opened the freezer door, removed the ice cream carton, and gently placed it down on the floor.

Lechuza

When her nephews would visit and they were
playing in the living room, they would suddenly
stop and look up. They would stare at the ceiling
for a while as if someone were there.

After Socorro's brother-in-law died in jail, he
would visit the house. Henri's five-year-old
grandson had reported seeing a male ghost in the
house.

Henri said, "Is he the one who yanks on my hair
when I try to sleep? Once, I was watching TV in
my bedroom with my back to the hallway and
sensed a presence behind me, so I quickly turned
around. Out of my peripheral vision I spied a man
coming up behind me with a knife. As soon as I
turned around completely, the man was gone. I
am convinced that this was the ghost of Socorro's
brother-in-law who was convicted of murdering
her in this house with a knife. With much prayer I
am convinced that he was banished from this
house."

She continued, "Another time, while fixing the
kitchen sink, I stepped away for a few minutes.
When I returned, all the tools and the new sink
parts had disappeared. I had to buy brand new
tools and repair parts. Finally, my new pet dog will
not sleep in my room. She is scared. Nor will she
go into the bedroom where Socorro died. This is
the room where my friend Hernán sensed a big

cold spot. I stayed at the threshold to this room while Hernán walked around."

"Henri," he said to me, "I sense a cold spot—wait," looking up at the ceiling he added, "It's nothing. I see the air conditioning vent. It's blowing cool air right on me."

Henri slowly shook her head in a negative gesture, "The air conditioning is not on."

Hernán then walked up to me and pointed at his arm. There was raised goose flesh on his forearm.

"Can we see the attic now?" Hernan asked?

He followed me up the stairs into the attic and examined the toys. They all seem innocuous, he observed. The red fire engine, however, was of special interest.

"Henri, is this the fire truck whose siren you hear around midnight?" Henri nodded. She had mentioned this story in the past.

"It seems entirely mechanical." He turned the red fire engine over in his hand adding, "I don't see a place to insert batteries?"

"We've had it for years, and as far as I know, it doesn't require batteries. The siren sounds when you push it around on the floor and the wheels turn."

"Only two sets of windows in the attic, Henri?"

"Yes," Henri replied."

Hernán observed that the only windows in the attic faced east and west.

"East toward the freeway," he said, "and west toward the end of your two-acre yard? Where does your backyard end?"

"There is a canal at the end of my backyard. My yard is fenced in though, and I keep the back gate locked."

"I see," Hernán replied, "Now can we see the basement?"

We went down the stairs and into the master bedroom. Henri pointed to what appeared to be a cabinet door between the entry door to the bedroom and the bathroom door.

"To the casual observer, it is just a cabinet door," Hernán observed, adding, "May I open it?"

Opening the door, darkness from within overwhelmed the observer. However, to the discerning eye, this entry door to the basement is too low to the floor and completely out of place. Who would put a cabinet door here unless it is merely for decor? However, the door is completely functional.

"I suspect, Henri," Hernán continued, "that there is at least one latch on the inside to secure the door once one is inside?"

"I don't know for sure, Hernán. I have never gone in."

"If you will let me Henri, I would like to go in, but it will have to be in a month's time, or so. I will have to return to Houston for some equipment. Better lights than I have with me. Heavy leather gloves, knee pads. As it is, I will have to crawl in that small decoy door. Once inside, I do not know if the basement is wired for lights. I don't know if it has an extremely low ceiling, or normal ceiling seven or eight feet high so that one can stand up once inside."

"What do you think you'll find inside?"

"I have some ideas Henri, about this basement and your attic. I think both were added on after the house was built. I do not think they were intended to serve as a normal attic or basement, but I will not know for sure until I explore the basement. I can tell you this, Henri, that attic was not added on as a normal attic."

116

Lechuza

"You think they just wanted an extra bedroom?"

"No Henri, at least I don't think they intended to use it as an extra bedroom. I am almost certain that it was added as an *atalaya*, that is, a lookout tower. Which is why, the only windows face the freeway and the canal, so that no one can sneak up on the house from the freeway or canal."

"And the basement?"

"The basement, Henri, I think is actually a safe-room, or what is more commonly known as a panic room. We will both know once I can get inside."

A few weeks after Hernán first visited the house, we spoke on the telephone.

"Hernán," Henri started, "I had my oldest son remove the door to the basement and sheetrock the opening."

"Why was this, Henri?"

"Well Hernán, my son went to high school with Georgie, Socorro's oldest son. They knew each other, and my son tells me that Georgie bragged that the basement was where his parents stashed their drugs until they could move them."

Henri continued, "Before removing the door, my son crawled inside. He described it as a box, perhaps eight-by-ten feet, with an exceptionally low ceiling, perhaps only four feet high. Additionally, my son informed me that it was completely empty."

"Of course, it is your house Henri, and you have every right to do what you did; however, I still wish I had checked the basement out myself. Naturally, I believe your son, but I may have spotted something he missed."

"Like what, Hernán?" Henri asked?

"Perhaps nothing Henri, but I may have found residue that could prove drugs were once stored there. Or perhaps even a secret trapdoor leading to another hidey-hole."

"Well, Hernán. I also spoke with a psychic who assured me that it was best not to dig any further. It could make things worse. She said that the spirits seem to have accepted me, but they would not be comfortable with a stranger snooping around. Anyway, the psychic added, anything that might be found in the house should be left alone whether it is drugs, money, or jewelry. Malignant spirits can attach themselves not only to places and people, but also to things. It's best to leave the past behind."

Lechuza

"The psychic also suggested that I try speaking to the spirits. She said to tell them to go into the light, that this house is no longer theirs."

Henri said, "I have often prayed, but until now, I never tried telling the spirits to go into the light. Since I had the basement door sealed, it has been so peaceful here. Even my little dog is no longer afraid to come into my bedroom with me."

"I am happy that you are at peace, Henri. Ultimately that is what really matters," Hernán said to her.

"When you are back in Edinburg, Hernán, call me. Maybe we can have coffee at I-Hop?"

"I'd like that Henri."

Lechuza

Chapter 11

Old McAllen Hospital

Henri Garza had another story to tell.

"The story which I am about to relate, Hernán," Henri began, "Occurred during 1991. I was in my thirties then, and I worked at the Boot Jack Western Wear store in McAllen, Texas, on East Jackson Avenue. One of my best friends was Felicia, who at the time was in her twenties."

Henri and I were at the I-Hop restaurant in McAllen sipping fresh coffee while Henri reminisced, and shared her ghostly encounter with me.

"Felicia," Henri continued, "waited on tables at an IHOP across the street from the Old McAllen Hospital. I frequently stopped by to visit with Felicia when her shift ended at midnight. We would take a table and had something light to eat, or just enjoyed a cup of coffee, while telling each other about our day. You know, small talk, what we now call *girl talk*. We knew a Municipal Policeman named Art, who moonlighted as night watchman at the old McAllen Hospital.

Lechuza

Some nights during his break, Art would join us at the IHOP. On one such night in October, Art assured Felicia and I, that the hospital was haunted.

According to Art, late at night, babies could be heard crying and patients moaning. Were these sounds remnants of a by-gone-era when people suffered and even died within the hospital? Did the walls somehow retain these chilling sounds only to play them back at random times after dark? If we did not believe him, Art added, we could make a round with him one night."

She continued with her story. "The old hospital was purchased by the City of McAllen to be converted into City Offices. One late October evening, Felicia and I decided to take Art up on his offer. So, after I got off work, we went looking for Art at the old hospital. I had to bring Jorge, my oldest son along. He was 15 years old then, and he was extremely excited to be coming with us. When we went looking for Art, it did not occur to us that it was already October 30th."

Jorge kept asking me, "Mom, Mom, what time is it?"

I glanced at my watch and said, "It's a quarter to midnight, Jorge."

"Art let us in. He locked the front door behind us and asked us to wait for him by the front door while he went out back for something in his car.

We were jittery and anxious to explore the haunted hospital, so we became impatient waiting for Art. Felicia and I decided to look around a little while we waited for Art.

"Mom, Mom," Jorge started again, "what time is it?"

"Jorge, I already told you." I glanced at my watch, moving my wrist around to catch light from the outside, "It's ten till midnight, Jorge."

It was never our intention to wander so far from the front door, but the corridors had ceiling lights on motion sensors which came on as we walked along. The long hospital corridors all looked alike, and before we knew it, we were completely turned around. Which way was the front door?

"Mom, Mom." Jorge again.

"It's just past midnight, Jorge."

"Oh boy," Jorge exclaimed.

Not only did we become separated from Art, but Felicia and I were hopelessly lost in the old hospital. All the rooms were dark.

Lechuza

The corridors were all the same. By the dim corridor light which bled into a room, Felicia and I witnessed chairs move of their own accord. The room itself was devoid of any human presence.

Jorge said he did not see anything, but he was looking elsewhere. We ran madly down endless corridors trying to find Art, or at least the front door to let ourselves out. It felt cold. Cold weather does not usually start this early in the Rio Grande Valley of Texas.

Exhausted from running for what seemed to us like miles, we considered stepping into one of the rooms to sit down.

"Not a good idea," Felicia said, "Only the corridors have lights and they stay on only so long as we keep moving."

"Mom," Jorge again, "I thought I saw a red ball of light behind us."

"It's just your imagination, son..."

We had not stopped for even five minutes when we heard subdued cries. Felicia and I stared wide-eyed at each other.

Jorge asked, "Mom, was that my imagination too?"

Lechuza

"Babies," I exclaimed! *"Felicia, Jorge... Those are babies crying!"*

"Again, we ran down the corridors unaware of where we were going. If we ran fast enough, and long enough, we would run into Art, or find the front door where we were supposed to be waiting for Art.

We paused again and now we could plainly hear the moans of old and sick people coming from the dark rooms. Where were we? Were we near the old trauma rooms, or the area where surgeries were performed? Were we near the patients' recovery rooms? I held on tightly to Jorge's hand. Somehow, we found the energy to continue running. What were we running from, ghosts or our own imagination? And where was Art? Why had we not run into him yet?

Suddenly we spied an orb of dull red light about the size of a volleyball, in the corridor, silently floating toward us. More frightened than ever, we ran like mad people away from the orb. Only Jorge seemed more excited than afraid.

We caught sight of the front door. Was the orb of red light nudging us in the right direction? We could distinguish a traffic light flashing red all around, just outside, through the glass front door. Was the orb really following us, or was it merely a projection from the flashing red traffic light?

125

More importantly, would the front door be locked? Still, we ran for the *light at the end of the tunnel*, hoping against hope that the door would somehow be unlocked.

We made a final, furious dash for the front door pushing against the metal bar that served as a door handle with our combined weight. The door swung open and the three of us were catapulted out. We did not waste any time running toward our car parked across the street where Felicia worked."

"Mom," Jorge again.

"It's almost 1:00 am, Jorge."

"No Mom, It's after midnight!"

"Yes Jorge, what about it?"

"It's after midnight, Mom. It's Halloween's day!"

Of course. No wonder Jorge was so excited!

The following evening, when we met up with Art, he was terribly upset with us because we left. He spent all night looking for us, not knowing what had happened.

"I was so worried about the three of you," Art said, "Where could you have gone in the dark?"

Lechuza

Felicia and I looked at each other.

"Art," I said, "The corridors were illuminated by the ceiling lights which came on when we walked under the motion sensors."

Art looked both of us eye-to-eye, "What do you mean? There are no lights. The entire building is off the grid. The stand-by generators have no fuel. That is why I went to my car to get my extra flashlight for you girls. It needed fresh batteries though and that is why I was gone so long. I had to find a convenience store that had D-size flashlight batteries."

Ψ

Lechuza

Chapter 12

The Death Cell

Circa mid-1800's, in the City of Durango, State of Durango, Mexico, the municipal jail had a singularly unique, prisoner's cell designated the *Death Cell*. It was not what today would be known as a death-row cell.

This was literally a cell where a prisoner would not survive even a single night. The prisoner unlucky enough to be placed in this cell would mysteriously die during the night. There were no exceptions. Any prisoner placed here, could not expect to see the morning light. For decades death would call upon the prisoner unfortunate enough to find himself in this accursed cell.

As to be expected, the jailers reserved this cell for problematic prisoners. For prisoner who, for whatever reason, were generally disliked among the guards. It was reserved for the dregs of society, the wife and child beaters, the mean drunks, those who resisted arrest and perhaps injured or killed one of the officers involved in the apprehension. No questions were asked. There were no appeals.

The outcome was always the same. In the morning when the death cell was opened, the undertaker and his assistant always accompanied the jailer to collect the dead prisoner. This protocol had been established years before.

Wrong or right, the death certificate always recorded *Natural Causes*, and the case was closed.

One day during 1884, a *pistolero* (a gunslinger) named Juan was arrested. He had been asked to destroy a dog afflicted with rabies, and somehow his bullet also killed a local woman. It is not known if the bullet was a ricochet, or a bullet that went through the dog and killed the woman, or if perhaps the woman inadvertently stepped between the dog and Juan as he fired the fatal shot. The result was the same, an innocent woman in the prime of life was dead and Juan was to blame.

Pistoleros like Juan were never well-thought of, and they were largely feared. They were considered violent and volatile men who would just as soon gun you down as talk to you. At least among *los campesinos*, (the country folk), Juan did not fit into that category.

He was considered hard-working with many friends, and even though his aim was good, and he was fast on the draw, he only resorted to gunplay as a last recourse and would only use his gun in defense of self or others.

Juan was incarcerated at the Durango Municipal jail and promptly placed in Cell 27, the notorious *Death Cell*. Were the stories true? Or were they just old wives' tales intended to make young people fearful of ending up in jail?

People used to say, "Act right *chamacos* (boys), do not get drunk, do not fight, do not gamble, do not cheat at cards, and do not hit women, or you shall go to jail. You could end up in Cell 27."

Juan knew of at least three men who were rumored to have been incarcerated in the Durango Death Cell: *El Diablio* Muñiz, a slight man who stayed drunk while his wife and children starved. The local priest once attempted to council him, and for his effort, he was beaten unconscious by *El Diablio*.

Then there was a man known only as El *Chango*. El Chango was dimwitted and rumored to possess incredible strength. What started out as a friendly arm-wrestling match in the local *cantina*, left one man with a severe fracture of his right arm. He was never able to work again. Five of the injured man's friends attempted to stop El Chango, and they were severely beaten.

Lechuza

And there was Don Elias Garcia, an older man who took a young bride. Don Elias was insanely jealous. His young bride simply vanished one day. Did he take her to a remote part of his extensive hacienda where he deposited her lifeless body in one of many abandoned wells? She was never seen again. Garcia was detained overnight for questioning. And like his young bride, he was never seen again.

Neither were the other two men. Crudely scrawled on the walls of the Death Cell Juan found the word *chango*, the initials DM, and EG, along with other names, initials, and doodles.

There could be no tolerance for a man who killed an innocent woman, even though Juan and several eyewitnesses testified that the woman's death had been accidental. By the following morning, Juan would surely be giving account to our Maker for firing the shot which led to the woman's death. It could not end any other way; Juan was under a sentence of death.

Imagine for a moment, being Juan. Unjustly incarcerated in a tiny jail cell. Three solid walls and a series of iron bars between you and freedom. A dirty brass pot to use when nature called. A filthy cot to sleep on as you waited for the morning that you knew would never come.

Lechuza

Early that morning in 1884, two jailers, the undertaker, and his assistant, reported to the Durango City Jail. They came prepared with a stretcher to remove Juan's lifeless body from the Death Cell. Surely destiny had once again spared the City of Durango the cost of a trial, as had been the case so many times in the past.

As the head-jailer turned the large brass key to open the Death Cell door, heavy tumblers loudly clicked into place, the sound reverberating off the cold, black stone walls. Everyone was astonished to see the prisoner rise from his cot in the jail cell. This was but their first surprise that morning.

Juan, very much alive, greeted the jail personnel with a cheerful, *Good morning,* and Juan proceeded to lift his *sombrero* from the jail floor.

Immediately the men recoiled in abject terror at what was trapped under Juan's hat. Now, all the men present were *Durangueses*, Citizens of the free and sovereign, State of Durango. Like all Citizens of Durango, they were keenly aware that even a single sting from the smallest Durango scorpion would inflict a very painful death in only a matter of hours. The scorpion Juan had trapped beneath his hat was nearly 18 centimeters long, (7+ inches!)

Juan stated that he remained awake and so around midnight, he was able to see the large scorpion materialize from a crack in the ceiling. He watched the scorpion meticulously crawl upside across the ceiling, and down the wall, then walk straight toward his bed. As the scorpion neared, staring at him with multiple turquoise-colored eyes that gleamed in the dark, Juan rapidly removed his hat and trapped the deadly arachnid. Only then did he go to sleep.

Long before, it had been decided by the jail officials, that if any prisoner survived the night in the Durango Death Cell, he would automatically be pardoned, and given his freedom. Divine providence had judged Juan not guilty of the woman's death. Who were the civilian authorities to rule otherwise? The Death Cell was renamed, *La Celda de San Juan*—St. John's Cell.

The scorpion from the Death Cell was preserved, then it was taken to Mexico City where it was placed on display in a Museum. There it can be seen to this very day. Juan, the Pistolero, also became known as, Juan Sin Miedo—Fearless John.

Lechuza

Chapter 13

¿Quién Sabe?

During the early Forties there was an oil and gas
lease behind the Greenhill Cemetery just outside
of Hebbronville, TX. Greenhill Cemetery is situated
just south off State Highway 359, which goes from
Hebbronville to Laredo. This lease came to be
known as the *Quién Sabe Lease,* and as far as I
know, it still bears that quaint and perplexing
name. For those who are familiar with the
language and regional colloquialisms, *Quién Sabe*
has a slightly ominous undertone, for this is what
the words mean: "Who knows?"

Now, no one would work the Quién Sabe for long.
The men who checked the meters and gauged the
flow from the oil and gas wells simply would quit
after working there for only a day or two. These
were hardened men accustomed to hard work and
not afraid of the elements or of the local wildlife.
Indeed, lesser men would blanch at the prospect
of working in the heat and dust and flee in terror
after encountering even a moderate sized
rattlesnake. Men who work these leases are
accustomed to being alone in the great outdoors
and treat threats of nature such as rattlesnakes

with impunity. When confronted with a large
rattlesnake, they will simply kill the snake, tan
the hide for a belt, and keep the rattler to decorate
their hats.

The problem at Quién Sabe appeared to be a
threat of nature, but the frightened men would
only speak in hushed whispers of... an animal of
some kind. Some would go as far as to speak of "A
huge bird," but none dared articulate what every
soul feared, *Lechuza*.

Schooled and learned people will tell you that a
lechuza is nothing more than a common barn owl.
In Spanish, an owl is also a *tecolote*, or a *buhó*,
and as a point of fact yes, a *lechuza* is an owl.
However, to those of us familiar with the *old ways,*
a lechuza is much more than just an ordinary owl.
On either side of that river we call the Rio Grande,
from Matamoros to El Paso del Norté, none will
utter the word *lechuza* to describe a common owl.
This word is always regulated to the dark side,
that place where ghosts, nightmares, and *demons*
dwell.

The *patrones* and the owners of the lease
despaired. They were losing income from the lack
of production. No one wanted to work the Quién
Sabe Lease.

The foreman for the oil and gas company told the
meter readers and those who gauged the flow,

"There is nothing to fear. You are outdoorsmen. Take your rifles with you when you work the Quién Sabe. If there is a problem with the local wildlife, take care of it!"

Reluctantly the men agreed to return to work. The next day, all the men told the *patron* that they were not returning to Quién Sabe. "What is the matter?" the puzzled supervisor and foreman demanded. "You took your rifles, did you not?"

"*Sí*," replied Tomás Garcia with his hat in his hands, his brown eyes lowered. He looked briefly at the other men before continuing. Then Tomás pointed at another man and said, "Francisco fired his .30-30 Winchester at the fiend!"

"You missed then," the *patron* hissed in disgust.

"No," Francisco insisted shaking his head, "I never miss, *patron*."

"Then what the hell happened?"

The men murmured among themselves all at once.

"It is true, *Patron*," Manuel Gonzalez insisted, "Francisco never misses. I have seen him drop a deer on the run with a single shot."

The foreman and supervisor stared at the crowd of men all nodding their heads in affirmation. "Then the beast is dead?"

"No boss, it did not die." Francisco lowered his eyes. "And I did not miss."

"Man, how can you say you shot it with a .30-30 and it did not die! It must be dead..."

"The fiend," Francisco stated, "spat the bullet back at me. And here it is." Francisco dropped a fired .30-30 bullet into the foreman's hand. He dropped it as if it were still too hot to handle. The men murmured loudly and dispersed before the supervisor or foreman could protest or try to convince them to remain on the job.

In desperation the company sent for a worker from Galveston, an anglo man who was not superstitious. He, too, stayed but one day.

"I'm ah headin' back to Galveston boss!" The man announced, "T'ain't natural what's goin' on round here!" And he got in his truck and drove nonstop six hours back to Galveston.

Many days passed, and it seemed that the Quién Sabe would have to be shut down for good. Not even outsiders wanted to work there.

Lechuza

One day a local man, Abel de Los Santos, spoke with the Quién Sabe foreman. "I need work," Abel said quietly, "and I am not afraid to work the Quién Sabe." He was hired immediately.

Early the following morning Abel kissed his beautiful wife Gloria goodbye. The night before he had loaded his father's old Remington 24E semi-automatic rifle behind the seat of his work truck. In the glove box was a new yellow box of .22 Long Rifles hollow point bullets. When Abel got to the local cemetery, he retrieved his rifle from behind the seat. Then he loaded ten bullets into the rifle, made sure the safety was on, and he chambered a round. He signed himself with the *sign of the cross* and drove into the Quién Sabe lease.

It was not long before Abel spied what had frightened all the other men before him. Perched on a fence post was the biggest owl Abel had ever seen. He knew even then that it was not a real owl, but a... *Lechuza*, for her eyes glowed red like hot embers.

Without leaving his truck Abel took his father's rifle and aimed at the Lechuza through the driver's side window. He fired his .22 at the large bird and heard his bullet strike the creature's breast with a dull thud. The huge owl extended its enormous wings and took to flight. Hurriedly Abel shut his driver's side window as the bird swooped down and spat the .22 bullet back at him. The bullet bounced harmlessly off the safety glass. Abel retreated to the cemetery reasoning that the creature would not follow him into consecrated ground.

Abel tested the rest of his bullets on tin cans. Each time his bullet thoroughly perforated the cans. "There is nothing wrong with my rifle or the bullets," Abel said to himself. "Now," he said under his breath, "I know what I must do!"

Abel drove into Mirando City some thirty miles west of the Quién Sabe Lease. There he met with the local Franciscan Priest at the St. Agnus Catholic Church.

"*Padrecito*," Abel began, "I need to make my confession..."

After the Priest heard Abel's confession, Abel asked the Priest to walk with him to his pickup truck, "Padre, I need one more favor...

Late that afternoon, around nightfall, Abel returned to the Quién Sabe. He soon spied the large owl with the glowing red eyes perched on the same fence post as before. Abel took careful aim and fired a single shot at the large bird. The bird toppled over at the sound of the shot.

Lechuza

Slowly Abel walked up to the fallen bird. "*Maldita bruja*," Abel said to the owl as he picked it up by a wing and hauled it back, throwing it into the bed of his truck. When he finished working Abel drove back home in the dark.

The following morning when Abel went to his truck, he found a woman shot in the shoulder where he had left the owl in the bed of his truck. The woman admitted that she was the Lechuza, explaining that she had been hired by the inheritors not included in the royalty pool of the Quien Sabe Lease.

"What did you shoot me with that my powers failed to protect me?" The woman demanded.

Abel solemnly replied, "Your powers are not greater than those of God. I had the *padrecito* bless my bullets and for good measure, I cut a cross into each one with my pocketknife!"

"Please do not kill me," the witch pleaded.

"I shall take you to the Sheriff. To him you will confess your crimes."

"NOOO! Please, they will not allow a witch to live. I have children. For my children I beg you! Let me live! I'll shall never trouble you again!"

"Where are you from?" Abel demanded.

"From Garceño, close to Roma..." the witch
replied.

"I know where that is," answered Abel. "That is
far enough away. Go back to your children and
never return."

Lechuza

Chapter 14

Headless Horseman of Coyanosa

Robert Salinas, Jr. was 16 years old when his family went to Coyanosa, Texas to work in the fields. In those days Coyanosa was a small town located a hundred-some-miles northwest of Ft. Worth, Texas, and some hundred-something-miles southwest of Oklahoma.

The people that the Salinas Family worked for, arranged for the workers to stay at some deserted barracks a couple of miles outside of the actual town of Coyanosa. The old barracks for the workers, made suitable living accommodations for the large group of itinerant workers. Outside the barracks Robert and his friends whiled away the days playing baseball until it was time to go to sleep. A single streetlight illuminated the playing field for Robert and his friends. Robert tells this story.

The workday started early and ended early. By ten or eleven in the morning, we would find ourselves playing non-stop baseball until it was time to drop off to sleep.

Lechuza

One evening while we played ball, I heard a horse
approach our playing field, clop, clop, clop, clop...
A curtain of shadows literally draped the world
beyond the tiny perimeter of safety which our
floodlight offered. A horse approached, clop, clop...
I paid little attention because it was not so
unusual then, for people to ride horses.

Yet a chill rolled up and down my spine when I
noticed a lone horseman dressed in dark clothing
that rode along the unlighted perimeter of our
playing field. Why did he stay just out of the light?
Only the dark silhouette of the horseman astride
the huge black horse was distinguishable in the
dead of night. Unhurriedly, the horseman rode
along. Abruptly, he stopped to observe us. There
he remained, perfectly motionless on his big black
horse, both hands on the saddle-horn, just
watching us play ball. Without warning the
horseman yanked the reins on his horse hard.

He rode at a hard gallop with both hands on the
reins, leaning forward in the saddle. Cloaked in
darkness he managed to stay just out of sight. We
saw the horse leap over a fence we knew was just
behind the barracks where we slept. *How strange,*
thought I, *the horse came down on the far side of
the fence without a sound?* Intent on the game I
did not concern myself with this until a day or two
later.

Lechuza

The following evening, I again heard the horseman approach. This time the dark rider was bolder and skirted well into the lighted playing field where all the players caught sight of him. *A trick of the light,* I thought, *or just the shadows,* for what I saw could not be. The horseman did not have a head. *It must be the shadows*, I rationalized fearfully. Again, the horseman hesitated just a moment at the same spot before galloping toward the fence. When the horse touched down on the far side of the barbed wire fence there was no sound at all. The next day we checked. To our astonishment we could follow the horse's tracks up until it jumped over the fence. On the far side of the fence there was... Nothing. The ground was softer there so the horse's hoof prints should have been evident, but there were none. We expressed our concerns to the grown-ups, but they did not really listen to us.

We knew something was not right about this mysterious horseman and so we made plans to get to the bottom of this mystery. The grownups were no help. They were much too busy or too concerned with other matters to listen to our concerns. A headless horseman, indeed! Left to our own devices we made up a story about how this was a special, big play-off game. And so, the grownups agreed to watch us play baseball that evening after dark.

Lechuza

Without saying anything we concealed big piles of
baseball-size rocks close to the place where we
knew the horseman and his horse would ride
through to bound over the fence as he did every
night. The rocks were just the right size to pelt at
the mysterious headless horseman. But what if he
did not appear now that we were ready for him?

Our parents watched the ball game, sitting on
their comfortable lawn chairs and sipping their
lemonade and ice teas. Then, about ten p.m., the
horseman came. He rode boldly across our playing
field astride his big, black horse. You could hear
the clamor from the adults. They rose suddenly.
Their iced tea and lemonade dropped to the
ground. Their lawn chairs all overturned. The
rider had no head.

As the grownups excitedly murmured, we grabbed
our rocks. As the horseman rode by us, we pelted
the rocks with force at the rider and his horse.
The rocks just went through the rider and his
horse as if they had no more substance than a
shadow. The grownups could doubt us no longer,
even though no one could explain what was
happening.

The weekend came and so the teenagers rode into
town for our weekend ritual burger and fries.

Lechuza

The manager approached our table, "Hey, aren't you the boys who are staying at the old cotton gin?"

"Sure, that's us," I replied with a big grin.

"Have you seen the horseman yet?"

You could have heard a pin drop. I managed to answer, "Yes sir, we've seen him."

"Let me finish fixing your burgers," the man winked at us and motioned with his big hand, "and I shall tell you the story of the *Headless Horseman of Coyanosa, Texas*."

After preparing our burgers and fries, the man served us and sat with us at our table. He began to speak.

"About thirty years ago, a man and his wife lived in those old barracks where you now live. This man was a fence rider for the ranch who would leave early every morning on horseback to mend fences by splicing wire or adding staples to the fence posts where needed. The rider did not return home until late in the afternoon.

One day, the rider forgot his lunch. At about ten that morning he unexpectedly returned home to find his wife with another man. A fight ensued, and his wife and her lover murdered the fence rider. In a panic the murderers dismembered his body and buried the different body parts in diverse places near your sleeping quarters.

Soon the fence rider was missed, and the local authorities launched an investigation into his disappearance. All the body parts were unearthed, and the unfaithful wife and her lover were convicted of his murder.

"Sir," Robert politely interrupted by raising his right hand, "You say that all the body parts were found?"

"Yep," the manager replied, "all the body parts were eventually found. All, that is, except for one."

"Except for what?" Robert nervously asked.

He paused to make eye contact with all the boys listening to the macabre story. "You see boys, one body part has never been found and so the fence rider still rides that big, black horse every night. He is looking to find his missing head. His head has *never* been found."

Chapter 15

Duende

My oldest brother, Hector, ran away from home when he was about 16. I was a young child when this happened, and so I barely remembered him.

I do recall hearing talk of the police coming to talk to my parents about my missing brother. When I was old enough to understand, I was told that Hector had been found dead, somewhere in Mexico. Since my parents did not have the money to send for the body, nor could they travel into Mexico to identify him, I assumed that he was buried in a pauper's grave.

Then one fine, bright, and sunny day, when Hector was in his early twenties, he came home. He was alive and well and had a wife and a young family to boot.

To this very day, we have no idea who the deceased person mistaken by the authorities for Hector was. All we know is that an unknown person rests in a pauper's grave somewhere in Mexico and that he was misidentified as my brother, Hector.

Lechuza

I did not enjoy much rapport with Hector until I
became a grown man and could afford to
communicate by long distance with him.

It seems that Hector had ended up in Quintana
Roo, Mexico, married there and had family. For a
living, Hector now piloted a fishing boat that
tourists in Cancun and *Isla de Mujeres* would
lease for the day. He did this until he retired
nearly in his eighties.

One day another brother of ours, Eustacio
Hinojosa-Canales (*Tacho*, as we called him), was
terminally ill with cancer in Pharr, Texas. To my
astonishment, Hector was in Pharr to see our
brother. Hector explained that the Red Cross had
obtained special permission and Visa for him to
visit our dying brother. I was now retired, and
having family in the Valley area, I arranged to
spend time there visiting my two brothers.

Tacho and I were fascinated listening to Hector tell
of his thrilling adventures on the high seas, and in
the jungles of Yucatan and Quintana Roo. Hector
told us of a *Llorona* (wailing woman) of the sea,
and that having tired of living on the beach, he
devoted some three years of his life to exploring
the jungles there. Most fascinating of all, he
spoke of finding some ruins, or *ruinas* in Spanish,
that he was nearly positive had not yet been
discovered by other white men.

150

Lechuza

Conversing with my brother Hector, I also learned that the local citizenry in Yucatan and Quintana Roo typically called the Pyramids and other ancient Mayan structures, *ruinas*.

One day, Hector told us that he asked the local people, "*Who built the ruinas?*"

Without exception the locals simply replied, "Los Jorobados," which is Spanish for, "The Hunchbacks."

Hector didn't keep us in suspense for long.

"One day," Hector said, "I was walking through the jungle down a well-worn foot path when I encountered a little man who was less than half my height. He wore simple earth-tone clothing, a red, brimless conical cap, and black boots. He had a full, neatly trimmed white beard, and he was a hunchback."

"This little man walked purposefully with both arms thrust across his chest. When I stepped directly into his path, he simply tried to walk around me. We did this silly little dance many times, and the little man never seemed upset with me. He simply tried to walk around me."

"Try as I did to engage him in conversation, it was an exercise in futility on my part. He totally ignored me. After about a half-an-hour of this

151

nonsense, I let the little fellow continue on his way. He walked away unhurried and unperturbed as if I had not even been a minor hindrance in his path."

Hector went on. "When I described this unusual encounter to my friends in Quintana Roo, they did not even seem surprised. They said that I had finally seen one of the *Jorobados* who built the ruins. And they never speak with regular people."

Did Hector describe an encounter with a *gnomo*, (gnome), or a *duende*; some kind of dwarf? Hector and I were approximately the same stature, 5 feet, 9 inches tall. This would make the little man my brother described *less than three feet tall!* Legends and fairytales are replete with stories of encounters with magical, diminutive people such as fairies, elves, pixies, sprites, imps, leprechauns, and such. Perhaps, if these beings do exist, they are not all evil and perhaps not all possess gold or precious stones to offer in exchange for being left alone.

Chapter 16

An Apocalyptic Story

An octogenarian lady named *Doña* Elvira Garcia was fond of telling the following story. It began something like this:

"There once was a man who lived in a town, not unlike this town. Indeed, it could have been any town in the Valley, but for the sake of our story, let us just say that it happened in *this* town.

A man would wait each night for his wife and children to go to sleep so that he could slip quietly out of bed to rendezvous with his mistress. The man would take a shortcut through an abandoned graveyard to meet his paramour.

Tonight, at the ancient graveyard, the man spied several strange lights. The lights resembled fireflies, which converged around a major light that seemed to rest atop an old tombstone. The smaller lights would approach this light, then fly rapidly away. When the man found the courage to venture closer, he discerned voices:

153

"In this town," said one of the fireflies to the Light, "is a man guilty of taking the Lord's name in vain. He makes sport of sin and never keeps holy the Lord's Day."

The major light decreed, "*Muerte repentina*— sudden death."

Another firefly approached, "In this town there is a man who neglects his family. He spends all of their money on drink while his children starve."

"Sudden death," the major light declared.

"In this *very* graveyard," a third firefly announced, "there is a man who makes a mockery of the *Sacrament of Matrimony*. He is guilty of the crime of adultery."

Before the major Light could pronounce sentence on this man, there before them appeared the Blessed Virgin Mary. Kneeling before the Light, the Blessed Mother begged to intercede on behalf of the guilty man.

"My Son," she began, "it is true that this man is guilty of the crime of adultery, however, he always remembers the Holy Family and frequently invokes their name, *Jesus, Mary and Joseph*. Give this man time to repent and amend his ways, my Son."

154

It is said that the Son will not refuse what his
Holy Mother asks of Him. Indeed, the first miracle
reported by the Christian New Testament,
changing the water into wine, was at the request
of the Mother of Jesus.

When seen from the point of view of the faithful,
this story ceases to be a fable, for is it not a basic
tenet of Judeo-Christian principle that the Lord
judges the living and the dead? One, however,
cannot seriously expect to go out to some old
graveyard late at night to witness Judgment Day.
I have often wondered if Doña Elvira knew that
she was telling an apocalyptic story.

The style in which the story is told is *apocalyptic*. It
is in the same genre as the *Book of Revelation*. Both
Revelation and this story, make bold use of exotic
symbolism to convey a text that is completely and
totally true. To decipher the meaning, one must
understand the symbolism. The symbolism of this
story can be interpreted in this manner:

The man who finds himself in an abandoned
graveyard during the dead of night is spiritually
dead. The only light in that place of darkness and
death is the Major Light who sits atop a
tombstone, for He truly is Master of Life and of
Death.

155

Lechuza

The minor lights, or fireflies, are spirits (or Angels, if you prefer) whose duty is to report the ills of the world to the Lord.

The other two men for whom no one interceded are also spiritually dead. It is important to understand that the Light did not execute these men, he merely *confirmed* their condition.

The man of the story, although dead in his sin, had one saving grace. He frequently invoked the name of the Holy Family, Jesus, Mary, and Joseph. Mary therefore interceded for him before her Son, buying him time to repent of his sins, amend his ways, and save his life.

The terrified man ran for his life back to his family. Never to return.

Chapter 17

To Trap a Witch

The prayer, *The Twelve Truths of The World*, is not recognized by the Roman Catholic Church. It is popular in some secular circles that traditionally use it as protection from witches.

According to Father Paul Chovanec, (St. Justin Martyr Catholic Church in Houston, Texas), it is possible that this prayer originated among a pious people who did not realize they were combining religious conviction *and* superstition in order to obtain magical results. Father Paul believes the prayer was created by necessity to deal with the fear of what they believed to be real.

The author wishes to thank Father Paul for his expertise and his most eloquent explanation into the possible origin of this prayer.

I then met with a woman by the name of Cecelia. She would recant this story regarding the prayer.

Lechuza

"I was the oldest of eight children," Cecelia began. "We were dirt poor, and lived outside of Mission, Texas about a mile from anywhere. Our Uncle Fidel, who was well-to-do, let us live on his acreage in a one-room, cinder-block building in a sugarcane field that was one of his many properties. The building kept the wind and rain out, but it had no plumbing nor was it wired for electricity. Mom cooked on a kerosene stove and at night we lit kerosene lamps to light our home."

Cecelia continued, "Dad drove a bus that transported *braceros*, (citrus grove workers), from the Rio Grande Valley of Texas to *el Norte* (North Texas), and sometimes out west to work. My brothers, sisters and I were kids at the time, and loved to munch on the sugarcane that grew in our uncle's field. When we had our fill of sugarcane, we would run over to the nearby citrus orchard to sample the tasty oranges and grapefruits that grew there. Although we were money-poor, we never went hungry, surrounded by citrus orchards and sugarcane fields as far as the eye could see.

That year our father was gone longer than usual, and after a few weeks mother began to worry. "*Anda rondando el mal*," Mom would say, "Something evil is out and about, I can feel it in the wind."

I was too young to understand what she was talking about, but her talk scared me. Mom kept a

158

pellet gun in the house that she used to shoot at the huge rats that always tried to get inside.

The block building that we lived in used to be a storage shed for corn, and I suppose that the rats thought it still had corn and so they tried to get inside. The rats made terrifying sounds at night, squealing, scratching, and scurrying around trying to get in. Mom would keep them at bay with her trusty pellet gun.

That night, after I had gone to bed, a violent wind and rainstorm began. Over the wind and clapping thunder, I thought I could discern a shrill whistling sound barely muffled by the rain slamming on our tin roof. Thunder pealed, and lightning flashed. Through the openings between the rafters in the unfinished ceiling, blinding flashes of lightning would momentarily light up the interior with an eerie, intense white light. During a lightning strike, I spied a dark shadow with huge, red glowing eyes that tried to insinuate its way into our home through an opening in the rafters. In the blinding darkness that followed I heard my mother whisper, "Something evil comes near..." I cowered beneath my blanket, shivering uncontrollably, afraid to even scream.

"It cannot enter," my mother reassured me from the darkness, "I sprinkled holy water to keep it out."

Lechuza

The following morning Uncle Fidel stopped by. Insecure in our poverty we were afraid that he was going to ask us to find some other place to live. He was a stern looking man, but in his own way he was kind and even generous.

Mom and our uncle talked for several minutes before we learned the reason for his visit. It seems that Uncle Fidel suffered some type of financial setback, and so he said to mother, "*Cuñada* (sister-in-law), we are going to have to go to *el norte* (the north) to work. We will be gone for a couple of months. I would really appreciate it if you and the kids would house-sit while we are gone."

That same afternoon we moved into our uncle's nice, brick house. Our uncle's house had its own water well and indoor plumbing. We did not have to worry about using an outhouse or having to shower outdoors with a garden hose. The only bleak note in our sudden turn of good fortune was that we still had not heard from our father. Now mother believed that something was seriously wrong.

"Something evil comes near," she stated once again, "it has followed us to your uncle's house."

160

Lechuza

One night I awoke from a deep slumber when I heard a shrill whistling sound that came from outside our window. Mother said that it was a *lechuza*, a *night witch* that had come stealing, coming nearer and nearer each night.

"Mother," I reasoned, "Mr. Fernandez, our sixth-grade science teacher, insists that *lechuzas* are just barn owls."

"Not this one, Cecelia," she assured me, "this one is a witch that wants to harm us."

Our uncle kept several genuinely nice hunting rifles in a gunroom in his house, but none of us knew how to use a firearm. Mom said that her pellet gun was useless against the evil creature that approached, coming nearer and nearer every night. I hoped against hope that father would return soon, but he remained gone.

"There are other ways to deal with a witch." Mom reassured me, "Mija, you are the oldest. I want you to fill this washbasin with water and set it in the middle of our bedroom."

I took the big, white washbasin mother handed me and filled it with water from the kitchen sink. Like she instructed, I returned and set it down right in the middle of our bedroom floor.

Lechuza

Mom nodded and said, "When the witch comes, I shall bring it down." I was really frightened. Mother seemed so grim.

"Bring it down?" I asked, "Mother, what do you mean?"

"I shall bring it down with the power of prayer, *mi'ja*, and this piece of rope."

"Mother showed me a thin piece of rope, long and flexible. "I shall recite '*Las Doce Verdades Del Mundo*,' she continued, "and for each truth of the world that I pray, I shall tie a knot in this rope. The *Lechuza* will be helpless and I shall learn who she is and what her intentions are."

"Mama, I am so afraid."

"Do not be afraid *mi'ja*, evil is not stronger than good and tonight I shall defeat this wicked thing once and for all."

"That night I was so frightened that I could not sleep. It was about midnight when I heard the strange, shrill whistling sound outside our window, closer now than ever. Mother always slept by the window and I heard mom scream as something slapped hard against the windowpane," Cecelia added.

"Mom," I yelled out in a panic, "What is wrong?"

Lechuza

"*Maldita lechuza,*" mom exclaimed, "that cursed witch has deafened me with the beating of her infernal wings."

"Oh mom, are you alright?"

"I'll be alright daughter, but she popped my left eardrum with her evil wing flapping."

"I did not ask mom how she knew that whatever slapped at our windowpane was a *she*, but mom seemed so certain. It was about two weeks before mom's hearing was back to normal. Once again, she readied herself with the washbasin filled with water and the piece of rope.

I was so frightened that night. Again, about midnight, the shrill whistling came stealing from the outside, a stealthy, steady sound that threatened to come inside our sanctuary. I ventured a peek from beneath my covers."

"Be quiet, mija," mom admonished, "She comes... Now!"

"I could see mom standing over the washbasin filled with water that sat on the floor, squarely in the middle of our bedroom. Mom was looking up, her face as if in a trance, the rope held firmly in her hands.

Lechuza

I was so afraid that I shut my eyes tightly. I could not see a thing, but I could hear everything that was going on."

Mom was praying, "*De las doce verdades del mundo decide una, buena hermana: Una es la Santa Casa de Jerusalem donde Jesucristo Crucificado vive y reyna por siempre y siempre, amen.*" (Of the Twelve Truths of The World good sister, say one—One is the Holy House in Jerusalem where Jesus Christ crucified lives and reigns forever and ever, Amen).

"*De las doce verdades del mundo buena hermana, decid la dos: La dos son las dos Tablas de Moises donde Dios dejo grabada su Divina Ley* (Of the Twelve Truths of The World good sister, say number two—Number two are the two stone Tablets of Moses where God inscribed His Divine Law...)"

"After each prayer I could picture my mother tying a knot in her rope, her strong fingers pulling the knot taut. The shrill whistling came again, but it sounded desperate, as if whatever had been stalking us all these many weeks now wished to escape but could not. Mom continued praying..."

"...The Third Truth of the World is the most Holy Trinity, Father, Son and Holy Spirit... The Fourth Truth of the world are the four Holy Evangelists, Mark, Luke, John and Matthew..."

164

Lechuza

"Mom continued reciting her prayer and the whistling was closer and more of a shriek than a whistle, closer than ever and somehow even more desperate. I dared not see what was happening in our own bedroom.

By the time my mother was reciting the Twelfth Truth of the world, the whistling had become a screech inside the room with us, a pathetic supplication for escape."

I heard my mother exclaim, "Look daughter, the *lechuza* has the face of a woman."

"I dared not look. I must have fainted because I do not remember what happened next, but in the morning, mother seemed very relaxed and at ease."

Smiling, mother said to me, "*Mi'ja*, your father will return today."

"I did not ask mom how she knew, but late that afternoon father's old, powder-blue twenty-four passenger, international bus pulled into the driveway.

Father had earned enough money to buy a small, frame house for us, out on Wisconsin Road. Happily, we moved there when our uncle and his family returned."

Lechuza

"Fidel," mother said to my uncle, "You won't be troubled at your home anymore. The malevolence is gone."

'We were never asked to house-sit Uncle Fidel's house again. Eventually Father was able to buy some acreage out on Morning Side Road. We moved our frame house to our new property, and we added rooms to it as our family grew. That was many years ago. I have often wondered what I would have seen that night, had I dared to open my eyes, perhaps a *night-witch* in the form of an owl with the face of a woman? I suppose that I really do not want to know."

Note from the Author

Traditionally, this prayer is used to trap witches. It is used with a length of rope on which a knot is tied after the recitation of each truth and continues until the witch falls from the sky helpless on the ground. The author does not vouch for its effectiveness nor does he endorse it. However, for the morbidly curious, it is listed verbatim on the following pages.
Best,
Hernán

XII Truths of The World:
By: Unknown

Of the Twelve Truths of The World, good brother, say number one:

Lechuza

One is the Holy House in Jerusalem where Jesus Christ
Crucified lives and reigns forever and ever, amen.
Of the twelve Truths of The World, good brother, say
number two:
Two are the two stone tablets of Moses where God
inscribed His Holy Law.
Of the Twelve Truths of The World, good brother, say
number Three:
Three is the Three Persons of the most Holy Trinity,
Father, Son and Holy Spirit.
Of the Twelve Truths of The World, good brother, say
number Four:
Four are the four Holy Evangelists, Mark, Luke, John,
and Matthew.
Of the Twelve Truths of The World, good brother, say
number Five:
Five are the Five Wounds on the Sacred Body of our
Lord Jesus Christ.
Of the Twelve Truths of The World, good brother, say
number Six:
Six are the six-candelabrum used to celebrate the High
Mass.
Of the Twelve Truths of The World, good brother, say
number Seven:
Seven are the Seven Words spoken by Jesus on the
Holy Cross.
Of the Twelve Truths of The World, good brother, say
number Eight:
Eight are The Eight Anguishes.
Of the Twelve Truths of the World, good brother, say
number Nine:
Nine are the Nine Months Jesus was in His most Holy
Virgin Mother's womb.

*Of the Twelve Truths of The World, good brother, say
number Ten:*
Ten are the Ten Commandments.
*Of the Twelve Truths of The World, good brother, say
number Eleven:*
*Eleven are the Eleven Virgins who assist at the Throne
of the Most Holy Trinity.*
*Of the Twelve Truths of The World, good brother, say
number Twelve:*
*Twelve are the Twelve Apostles who accompanied our
Lord Jesus Christ during His public life until His Death
on the Cross on Mt. Calvary.*
*Then the prayer continues by reciting the Twelve Truths
in reverse order:*
The Twelve Apostles,
The Eleven Virgins,
The Ten Commandments,
The Nine Months,
The Eight Anguishes,
The Seven Words,
The Six Candelabrum,
The Five Wounds,
The Four Holy Evangelists,
The Three Divine Persons,
The Two Stone Tablets of Moses,
*And the Holy House in Jerusalem where Jesus Christ
Crucified lives and reigns forever and ever, amen.*

Chapter 18

The Vanishing Hitchhikers

In the Winter of 1939, my father was driving from
El Tordio Ranch to the White Ranch one cold,
drizzly day in November. On the road he saw a
woman with three small children soliciting a ride.
The woman and children were huddled together to
keep warm. She was a sad, very pale young
woman with long, coal black hair.

They were barely dressed for the weather, the
woman in a plain cotton dress and shawl and her
children wearing light coats.
Dad was not in his pickup truck but in a
borrowed car that day, so he had room for four.
He stopped and asked the woman if she needed a
lift.

The woman looked at Dad with sad brown eyes
and answered, "Yes, please my children are cold."

"Sure, get in and warm up."

The woman and her children got into the backseat
of the car and after driving a short distance Dad
asked the woman where they were going.

169

Lechuza

"Can you leave us just before we get into Hebbronville?"

"No problem," Dad replied.

As they approached the town, Dad started slowing down and pulling over to the right shoulder.

"Are you sure this is as far as I can take you?" Dad asked, turning around to face the woman and her children in the backseat.

There was no reply. Dad stopped his car and looked into the backseat again. They were gone. They had vanished somewhere between where he had picked them up and the outskirts of Hebbronville.

It was just then that Dad noticed the Greenhill Cemetery off to the right where he had stopped. Was this where they had intended to go all along? He did not wait around to find out!

ψ

Chapter 19

Blood Rain

Many of my hometown friends found it hard to believe that I was actually a street cop in Houston, Texas. A good friend who recently retired from a South Texas Sheriff's Office once told me that he frequently had to correct our friends who were incredulous about my status as an actual street cop in Houston.

"He's a dispatcher," he was frequently told by mutual friends. "No," my friend Deputy Sheriff Leonel Herrera, now retired, replied, "He is a patrolman."

"No," some would argue, "I heard he didn't make it in Houston and that he's back in Laredo—"

"He's in Houston," Leonel would reply.

After this, when hometown people asked me, "What do you do in Houston? Aren't you a dispatcher?"

I'd say, "It's kind of hard to explain what I do in Houston, but if you really want to know, you can come up one day and I'll get you authorization to ride along with me. You will have to sign a waiver that says you will help me if I get in a bind, and that you will not sue our department if you get hurt. Every ride-along has to sign a release, that's just standard procedure."

Each time my friends would stare at me incredulously and wide-eyed. Not sure what I did growing up with them, but for some reason they could not believe I was a cop.

After a few seconds I would add, "Or, you can ask our friend Buck Hamilton what I do. Buck rides with me every chance he gets. In fact, my department likes Buck so well that he has been offered a job as an officer and helicopter pilot should he want to move up to Houston." George "Buck" Hamilton was a helicopter pilot, deputy sheriff, and a longtime friend.

Eventually, my friends changed their line of questioning to, "What's it like working for a large Police Department in East Texas? Or "Which was the most interesting case you ever worked?"

Truthfully, something interesting happened every day. Something incredible would occur, and then I would forget because something even more interesting would happen.

Lechuza

One Fourth of July evening, ten officers from our
platoon, along with two sergeants, were assigned
to crowd control at a fireworks show. The rest of
the platoon was assigned to freeway management
and answering calls for help.

I, along with Officer Cirilia Salas and Officer
Luther Odem, were assigned to the fireworks
detail. Cirilia and I were used to working together.
I was a senior officer, and Cirilia, somewhat of a
rookie then, knew she could count on me no
matter what. Luther was also a senior officer, and
despite our occasional differences in opinion, we
also worked well together. It was only natural that
we would back each other up when we were
working the same area.

No one expected trouble that evening, so we only
had our standard equipment, a 9mm duty
sidearm (I carried a 10mm Glock on-duty), our
expandable ASP batons, two or more pairs of
handcuffs, and of course, our ballistic vests.
Officer Odem was qualified with a 12-gauge pump
shotgun which he kept in the trunk of his patrol
car. I was the only officer present who was
qualified with, and carried a TAZER, which is a
less-than-lethal, electric-stun weapon.

Without warning, a riot involving approximately
5,000 spectators broke out when the fireworks
were delayed due to technical difficulties. The

three of us quickly ran to Officer Odem's patrol car to retrieve his shotgun.

The rest of the officers grouped up in threes and twos and stayed together for safety reasons. We marched through the crowd feeling very much like the Texans and the Texicans must have felt in 1836, at the Battle of The Alamo, as we ordered the rioters to disperse and go home. With only a dozen officers at the scene, attempting arrests was completely out of the question, if not extremely dangerous.

Twelve against five thousand, those odds just did not make any sense. But none of us backed down, none of us shirked our responsibilities, and none of us ran and hid. It was only by the Grace of God and perhaps the mere boldness of our presence which permitted us to maintain some type of order.

A lot of property damage was done that evening, and there were many minor injuries. There was one reported auto-pedestrian accident with minor injuries when one young man, running backward, (while throwing punches with both fists at his pursuers), ran into the side of a passing automobile. I volunteered to investigate that accident after we brought the rioting under control.

Lechuza

It was nearly an hour before we received
additional backup from other agencies.

It was a holiday weekend, and every agency had
their hands full. Again, it was the Grace of God
that no one was killed or seriously injured.

Even though Sgt. Eva Leclerc put the entire platoon
in for recognition, the Fourth of July incident went
down in the annals of the Houston Metro Police as
just, *business as usual.*

Another day, I was assigned to the Katy Frwy. (I-
10 West). Half-way through the shift I drove under
a pedestrian bridge which crosses over all lanes of
the freeway.

It was a cold evening and a heavy drizzle was
coming down with a vengeance. The drizzle was
heavy enough that I had to keep my wipers on,
but as I drove westbound under the catwalk,
heavy red drops fell on my windshield. I
immediately realized that these droplets, because
of their color and viscosity, had to be drops of
blood. Highly likely, human blood.

As I exited the freeway, I radioed in that I would
be off the freeway and out of my patrol car

Lechuza

investigating the source of the blood-rain over the Katy Freeway.

Our dispatcher, Lisa Barrera, informed me that citizens were already calling in reports of *blood-rain* at that very location. I was relieved to realize that I was not imagining things. The drizzle was hard enough to obliterate the blood-evidence before I pulled into the bus transit center to continue my investigation. If the blood were not coming from the pedestrian bridge, how would I be able to explain why I reported blood-rain on an official police channel?

The possible consequences ran through my mind and they were not pleasant: Days off? Psychological evaluation? Declared unfit for duty? Possible termination? Or none of the above?

I parked my patrol car and made my way toward the catwalk. I noted that it was as I thought, the blood-evidence on my unit had already washed away.

As I neared the catwalk, I could see three men squatting down on the walkway, hovering over another man who was flat-on-his stomach, stretched out on the walkway.

"Lisa," I called our dispatcher on my handheld radio, "start an ambulance to the Northwest Transit Center. Tell them that they'll see my patrol car and that I'll be on the cat-walk with an injured male." The three men giving first aid to the injured man quickly apprised me of the situation.

They did not know who the injured man was, but they knew that he was coming out of a half-way-house. Suddenly, the man went into convulsions and had fallen on his face on the catwalk.

Apparently, the fall knocked him unconscious. He was breathing but unresponsive. I removed my police jacket and covered him with it. The witnesses had already applied a makeshift compress which was soaked through with blood. I updated Lisa in dispatch and proceeded to jot down the witness's names and information, thanked them, and dismissed them. The ambulance arrived in a timely fashion, and the EMTs placed a compress on the man's head to stop the bleeding. He had a nasty gash and he did not regain consciousness during the time that we were at the transit center.

The Chief EMT informed me that the injured man's vitals were good and that he would probably recover. Without any further delay, the ambulance transported the man to the Ben Taub Hospital Emergency Room for further treatment.

This apparent fortean event, *blood-rain*, had a perfectly natural explanation. Can other Fortean

events be explained just as easily? Who can say?
Some things may not be for us to understand.

Chapter 20

The Donkey at Calvary

An old cowboy friend and *compadre*, Roel Cremar, once told me this story about how the *Blessed Virgin Mary Mother of Jesus*, made the 70-mile journey from Nazareth to Bethlehem on a donkey. I am very fond of his story because it explains several things of which many people may be unaware. It's an unusual sort of story than the rest you've read so far.

My wife and I met Roel January 1,1980. We later became *compadres* when we baptized and confirmed two of his boys.

We had just closed on our first house in Bruni, a small town in South Texas. Bruni, at any given time, boasts of an actual population between 250 to 500 residents. The Cremars lived across the street from our new house on Ave. B.

One morning my wife, Linda, asked me to go into our backyard and string up a cloth line so that we could air-dry our laundry. At the time we owned a washing machine, but not a working dryer. I knew that there were two large T-shaped steel posts in our backyard ideal for stringing a cloth line. Imagine my surprise when I walked into our backyard, to find sturdy wire already strung between the T- posts.

My wife wanted to know why I had returned so quickly from my assigned task and asked me, "Do you need help?"

"Ah, no," I replied, "There is clothesline out there ready to use."

We both walked out back and puzzled over who could have strung the clothesline for us. "Some nice neighbor," we speculated and left it at that.

That same afternoon, the Cremars walked over to welcome us. Mrs. Bebe Cremar brought some homemade *pan-de-polvo* (cinnamon sugar cookies). Mr. Cremar had an infectious smile as he doffed his cowboy hat and made the introduction and welcome, "We're your neighbors from across the street. Welcome."

Mr. Roel Cremar asked me if I was Tito Moreno's son."

"Yes," I replied, "he passed away some years ago."

"I am sorry to hear that; he was a good man. We were great friends back in the old days. In fact, I used to help him herd his cattle when it was time to take them to auction."

I vaguely recalled Papa Tito speak of a Mr. Cremar who was a good cowboy and an old *compadre* of his. I asked Mr. Cremar if they were *compadres*.

"Yes, we were," Mr. Cremar replied.

Our friendship was now set in stone.

For Christmas, *Compadre* Roel had received a new .243 Winchester Model 70 deer rifle from his children. It came equipped with a 4X scope and he worried about getting the scope set.

"Don't worry *Compadre*," I said to him, "I can set the scope for you."

"Well, the bigger problem is that I don't have anywhere to shoot."

"What's wrong with my place in Brooks County?"

"Oh," *Compadre* Roel exclaimed, "you must have inherited Maria and Tito's ranch."

That same afternoon, we drove the 38 miles from Bruni to my small Brooks County property to sight in his new rifle. Since it was just after the Christmas Season, *Compadre* Roel begin telling me the story of Nestor, the Donkey at Cavalry.

"As you probably know from the New Testament," *Compadre* Roel begin, "In those days, Caesar Augustus ordered a census of the whole world. Joseph and Mary had to go up from Nazareth in Galilee, to Judea, to the town of Bethlehem, because they belonged to the line and town of David. Mary was with child, and so it was not possible for them to walk the 70-some-miles from Nazareth to Bethlehem.

181

Joseph was a carpenter by trade and work had
been scarce. He took inventory of the few coins
they had saved up in a small, clay pot. There were
several minor copper coins which should be
enough to pay for food along their journey, and a
few silver shekels. Not enough money to purchase
a horse for Mary to ride, but perhaps a mule was
not out of the question. Mules are very sure-footed
and nearly as comfortable to ride as a horse.
Joseph and Mary proceeded to go see Jake Al-
Kaeé, the local horse, mule, and donkey monger.

"Three tyrian silver shekels," Jake told Joseph,
"will buy you this fine mule for Mary to ride
comfortably into Bethlehem. It is a special price to
you from me, purely out of human consideration
for your wife's delicate condition. If you wish,
when you return, I shall give you one silver shekel
for the mule. Provided, of course, that she is in the
same fine condition that she is now!"

But Molly the Mule would have none-of-that. She
was not about to trot all the way to Bethlehem,
with the pregnant woman on her back. Indeed!
And then have to return to Galilee with the
woman and child on her back! Rather than let
Mary ride her, Molly attempted to kick Mother
Mary.

Straightaway, like white lightning, a little donkey
came charging out of nowhere, braying and
snapping his jaws, threatening to bite Molly the
Mule. After chasing the mule, a safe distance from

182

Lechuza

Mary, the little donkey looked at Mary with compassion as if to say, "Do not worry Mary, I, Nestor shall carry you safely to Bethlehem and bring you back to Galilee!"

Mother Mary looked at Molly and said, "You had no compassion for a woman with child, and so you shall not bear any off-springs of your own until the *End Times*, when my Son returns."

Jake could not apologize enough to Joseph and Mary. "If you wish Joseph," he offered, "I can let you have Nestor for only two tyrian shekels. That is a true bargain, Joseph. Nestor is small for a beast-of-burden, but he is young and strong, and should accomplish the task you have in mind."

He continued, "I accepted Nestor in trade along with some coins, for a larger burro intending to sell him to someone with small children. Nestor likes children..."

Compadre Roel finished his story, "And so, this is how Mother Mary rode into Bethlehem on a donkey."

"So, *Compadre* Roel, is this why mules can't produce any off-springs?"

Roel smiled and added, "In a word, and without counting chromosomes, yes; but there is more. I have been a cowboy all my life. People literally fear the day when a mule will bear a colt. And I have seen times when a mule has been found nursing a new-born colt."

"So, it's happened?" I asked.

"No. If we look around a little, we'll find a mare looking for her lost colt. Mules cannot bear any offspring of their own, but they will kidnap newborn colts from careless mares, or adopt them if the mother dies while giving birth. What is incredible is that the mule will even produce milk to nurse her foster colt."

However, this is not where the story of Nestor ends. Remember how the New Testaments tells us that Jesus rode a white donkey triumphantly into Jerusalem? That donkey was Nestor. And Nestor was also there during the crucifixion, mourning the death of his dear friend Jesus. It is said that the shadow of the Cross of Jesus fell across Nestor's back. And Jesus rewarded Nestor for his friendship and faithfulness with an incredibly special gift. You see, to this very day, donkeys of Nestor's line bear the image of the Cross of Christ on their backs. In a manner of speaking, Nestor the Christmas Donkey is still with us, even today.

ψ

ψ

Chapter 21

The Dog That Nobody Wanted

She was only eight months old when someone dumped her on a deserted county road close to my country home. Scared and hungry she arrived at my front door.

At first, I mistook her for a female coyote. She was the right size to be a coyote and the right color. I assumed she was a coy-dog mix because she was in the submissive position for dogs trying to make friends with humans. Flat on her spine, paws up, and tail sweeping the ground. I gave her water and when I returned from work that evening, I fed her some table scraps and an old can of dog food.

That same evening, I went into town for a six-pack of beer, and a few cans of dog food. I had already started calling her *Missy*, and just added the *coyote* because, well, she looked like a coyote. After two or three weeks, when I realized that Missy Coyote was willing to stay, I decided to take her to the veterinarian. The lady Vet squealed with delight, "She's a full-blooded Red Heeler and she is beautiful." I already knew that Missy was beautiful, but I did not have any idea what a Red Heeler was. The Vet aged her by her teeth and informed me that she was eight months old. I had no idea that Red Heelers even existed, until I met

Lechuza

Missy Coyote and the vet informed me that she was a Red Heeler.

I asked the Vet to give Missy her shots and the anti-snake bite shots. It seemed I was shooting rattlesnakes nearly every day, and if she was going to be my ranch dog, I wanted her to have every possible chance to survive.

"If Missy should be snake-bit," the Vet explained, "bring her in for a booster, and unless it is a very severe snakebite, she should recover." I paid and walked out with Missy, her dog tags in my hand. Missy seemed incredibly happy, as if she knew she was finally accepted.

At the Family Dollar store I bought a bright green, broad nylon dog collar and affixed her dog tags with my phone number on them. I did not want her mistaken for a coyote or a stray and getting shot.

Missy became comfortable at my ranch. Missy would swim in my fishing pond, about an acre-and-a-half in size, from bank to bank every morning and evening, even when it was cold.

Soon, she started dragging home all kinds of debris; cans, bottles, old shoes—these things were her little treasures that I could not let her keep. I tired of picking up after her. As the days became warmer, she dug huge holes in the ground to cool off. These holes were a little too close to home, and too much of a stumbling-hazard for me as I aged not-so-gracefully. She was still young enough to be adopted and she was rapidly becoming a handful. I was finding holes in the ground to cover up, and debris to dispose of.

Driving home one dark, moon-less night, I decided that I would take Missy to the SPCA in the next few days. Missy would visit the neighbor's ranch when I left overnight, so I was really surprised to see her home this night. As I got off my vehicle, Missy immediately threw herself on my feet literally not allowing me to raise either foot. I reprimanded her and she let me take one small step. Then she whimpered and threw herself on my feet again. I scolded her and again she let me take another small step and she whimpered even louder and more piteously. Missy's actions were repeated five times before I heard a sound in the darkness just ahead and slightly to the left of my front door. Could it be? Yes, the distinctive rattling warning of a mature Western Diamondback rattlesnake!

Slowly I retreated to my truck. In the glove box I kept a flashlight and my .357 Magnum revolver. I brandished my flashlight and sure enough there, right by my front door, where months earlier Missy waited, was a mature, over five-foot-long

rattler in the ready-to-strike "S" position. Missy
stayed between me and the deadly snake. I was in
awe of her courage. She knew the rattler was there
and likely waited to warn me when I returned. She
could not know that I had her vaccinated against
the venom of the deadly Western Diamondback
rattlesnake. Still, she stayed between me and the
rattler until I dispatched the deadly snake with my
revolver. At the sounds of the shots Missy fled into
the darkness. She promptly returned safe and
sound when I called her name. Missy Coyote
finally found her forever home!

Chapter 22

Witch Owl

Roberto Corona was an ordinary man not given to
excesses. Having served honorably in Korea he
was awarded the first mail carrier's job when the
local post office started having home mail delivery.
He worked five days out of the week, like
everybody else, and went home to mind his own
business.

On days of obligation he attended Mass like
everyone did in this small South Texas town. He
would then retire to his small frame house on the
outskirts of town. Except for a new AM radio, to
keep him abreast of the news, his home was
sparsely furnished, his kitchen appliances old but
functional, and his house well-kept and clean. In
his spare time, he hoed weeds around his yard
and even though he could not keep grass in his
dirt yard, the soil too worn and infertile to sustain
carpet grass, he watered the trees that grew there.

Once a month he would buy a ten-pound sack of
chicken feed from the local feed store. He did not
keep chickens, but he would leave handfuls of the
feed at the base of the ancient *huisache* (sweet
acacia tree) that grew in his backyard.

One day he noticed Pingo, the neighbor's old, black and white Tomcat, stalking the red Cardinals that were on the ground eating the chicken feed. Roberto rushed out the back door slamming the screen door behind him.

Pingo stopped, his tail stretched straight out, and his right front paw suspended in midair. Foiled! Just three feet short of the first Cardinal! Pingo stared back at Roberto with yellowish green eyes and hissed.

"Pingo," Roberto yelled, "you bad cat! *Doña* Luz gives you plenty of table scraps to eat." Looking on the ground Roberto spotted a *caliche* rock about the size of a small orange. Quickly he grabbed the rock.

Pingo, perhaps seeing what was coming, quickly lost interest in the scrawny cardinal, and scrambled for the weathered-board fence that separated his mistress' house from Roberto's house. As Pingo clambered up the fence, cat claws digging vigorously into weathered wood, Roberto tossed the rock underhand. The rock harmlessly grazed Pingo and bounced off the boards with a resounding thud. Pingo spat and hurled over the fence. By this time, the Cardinals had safely taken to flight.

From that day, Roberto stopped throwing bird feed on the ground for the songbirds that visited his backyard. At the grocery store he purchased half a dozen large, ripe coconuts. With a hacksaw he opened holes at both ends of each coconut. He then drove a finishing nail into the middle of the coconuts and twisted a piece of wire to the nail. From the wire he suspended the coconuts, filled with bird feed, from the upper limbs of the *huisache* tree.

Roberto smiled at his handiwork, "Let Pingo try to get to the birds now."

From his side of the fence, Pingo stared at Roberto and bared his needle-sharp fangs. Before Roberto could see him, he turned tail and scrambled down the wooden fence, ran up the porch of his mistress' house and raced inside through the hole in the front door that served as a pet door.

One day Roberto stopped by Julio's feed store in town to buy his usual, ten-pound sack of chicken feed. "Mr. Corona," Blanca Patricia, the pretty cashier said, "I am sorry. We are all out of the ten-pound size."

Roberto thought for a moment. Autumn was already here, and the birds really needed to feed.

"I didn't know you kept chickens, Mr. Corona?"

"I don't Blanca. I do not keep chickens. I like to feed the songbirds that visit my backyard."

Instantly Blanca flashed a brilliant smile, "How kind of you, sir; I can give you an exceptionally good price on twenty-five pounds of cracked corn? Birds love to eat cracked corn."

"I suppose that will do, Blanca." Just to make conversation he added, "I made birdfeeders out of coconut husks that I hang from the trees so that my neighbor's cat won't bother the birds when they feed."

"You don't mean Pingo, *Doña* Luz's cat?"

Roberto stared at Blanca for a moment. "Yes. I didn't know that old Tomcat was so well known."

Blanca shivered, "That cat is evil. He scratched Paquito, my Beagle puppy, on the nose one day. Paco became extremely sick and nearly died."

Roberto smiled, "Blanca, sometimes dogs and cats don't get along. Your puppy probably frightened that old Tomcat—"

"No, Mr. Corona," Blanca persisted. She looked quickly around before leaning forward and whispering, "People say *Doña* Luz is a witch."

Roberto stifled a laugh, "I am sorry, Blanca, I don't mean to laugh; but to think that harmless old woman is a witch..."

"Mr. Corona," Blanca stared, her big brown eyes wide with apprehension, "you don't know what happened to her husband?"

"I didn't know she had a husband."

Blanca looked around quickly, "He was my father's best friend, but he drank too much. *Doña* Luz finally tired of him coming home drunk every weekend. He died in his bed. The Sheriff found a *coralillo*—a venomous Coral snake under his blanket. Sheriff Martinez tried to prove that *Doña* Luz had placed the snake in bed with him when she tucked him in drunk that night."

"I heard some such talk before I went into the Army, but the sheriff was never able to prove anything?"

"Mr. Corona, why do you think *Doña* Luz keeps a cat?"

Roberto stared at Blanca for a moment, "You're not going to tell me, *because she is a witch*?"

Blanca blinked, "Yes—no! I mean, of course she is a witch, but cats keep snakes away. That is why people keep cats around here! Even a Coral snake is afraid of that *Pingo*!"

Roberto smiled pleasantly; merely talking to such a pretty girl had already brightened his day. "Like always Blanca, it has been a pleasure talking to you." Roberto laid a couple of dollars on the counter for the cracked corn, collected his change and bid Blanca farewell.

Roberto got home and took out a piece of meat from the refrigerator to cook for dinner. He turned on his radio for the news and went to the kitchen sink to wash his hands.

From his kitchen window he noticed that there were not any birds in the *huisache* out back. From under the sink he retrieved the empty, five-pound coffee can that he used to fill the bird feeders. He filled the can with cracked corn and retrieved his eight-foot, wooden stepladder. Carrying the ladder and cracked corn out back he stopped dead in his tracks midway to the tree.

On the ground was Pingo with a dead cardinal in his mouth. Pingo stared back at him, making a menacing sound from deep within his throat. Before Roberto could react, the cat scrambled over the fence. Roberto was shocked as he surveyed his backyard. There were six dead cardinals on the ground.

Lechuza

Roberto ran around to his neighbor's house. As he stepped onto *Doña* Luz's front porch Roberto could see a trail of fine red feathers, which led straight to the hole that Pingo used as a pet door.

"*Doña* Luz," Roberto yelled, beating on her front door, "*Doña* Luz."

"*¿Que quieres?*" A voice echoed from inside, "What do you want?"

"Open the door," Roberto insisted, "we have to talk about your cat!"

An old lady opened the front door. She was hunched over with age, her hair was completely white, and she had *nubes* in her right eye—that is, her right eye was opaque with a cloudy film—cataracts.

"Who are you?" The old woman demanded.

"I am your neighbor, Roberto Corona. Your cat was in my back yard and he killed the cardinals that live there."

"How can you say that? Pingo is a good cat. He never gets into mischief. Besides, how can he kill birds that can fly away from him?"

"*Los ligo*—he must have mesmerized them the way cats or snakes do. There are six dead birds in my

backyard. That is more than he can eat. Keep
him out of my backyard, *Doña* Luz. I do not want
to see that bad cat there again. Good day!"

Roberto went back home and gathered the dead
birds. He placed all six in a brown paper sack and
he decided to dig a hole later that evening, when it
was cooler, to bury the birds deep enough that
Pingo could not dig them up.

He realized that he still needed to fill the bird
feeders, so he set up his step ladder and climbed
to the first feeder with his coffee can full of
cracked corn. "What is this?" Roberto exclaimed
aloud, "*¡Arroz crudo!* Someone put raw rice in this
feeder!" All six feeders had rice in them! Who
would do such a thing? Birds are unable to digest
rice. It swells in their craw when they drink water.
That's what killed them!

Roberto carefully collected the rice in another
paper sack, which he threw away. Perhaps
whoever put rice in the feeders did not realize it
would kill the birds? But why would anyone come
into his backyard to fill the feeders? He finished
filling the feeders with cracked corn and he went
back inside his house.

That evening about six o'clock, as he was
preparing to go outside to bury the dead
cardinals, he heard a car pull up by the front of

his house. To his surprise it was Sheriff Able Martinez.

"Evening Sheriff," Roberto greeted, "What can I do for you?"

"Mr. Corona," the Sheriff announced apologetically, "I am afraid your neighbor has complained about you mistreating Pingo, her pet cat."

"Sheriff, let me show you something." Roberto took the paper sack from the ground, opened it, and showed it to the sheriff.

"*Brujeria*," the sheriff announced with just a tinge of alarm in his voice. "I am afraid you have made a bad enemy, Mr. Corona, one I cannot protect you from. I am sorry, sir. Have a good day." With that the sheriff turned away, got into his car, and gunned the engine. A swirling contrail of flying gravel spewed from the back tires as he made a sharp U-turn and left in the same direction he had come from.

That night, Roberto had a dream where his Grandmother Maria was telling him about *lechuzas*.

"They are witches, *mijo*, who can change into owls." His grandmother told him as he sat on her lap.

"As owls," his grandmother continued, "they leave powders and potions and other awful things that harm their neighbors."

Roberto awoke soaked in a cold sweat. *¡El arroz crudo!* Now he knew how the rice got into the bird feeders!

That afternoon Roberto went to church to see the *padre*.

"Roberto," the old Franciscan Friar, Father Juniper, who greeted him cheerfully, "It is good to see you. What brings you to the Lord's house during a weekday?"

"Father," Roberto asked, not even daring to make eye contact with the old priest, "what can you tell me about... *lechuzas*?"

The old *padre* gave Roberto a puzzled look. "Why they are nocturnal birds, owls; why do you ask?"

Now Roberto stared directly into the priest's eyes, pleading. "They are *not* witches that can become owls, Father?"

Lechuza

The old priest paused before replying. "There are stories," he said hesitantly, "*cuentos*—tales that old people tell, of evil persons who change into some unseemly creature. Wolves, bats, owls to name a few; but those are myths, my son."

"Then a witch cannot become an owl?"

Again, the old *padre* hesitated. He rose laboriously to his full height, sighed, and turned away. Then he sat back down and calmly continued. "All along the Rio Grande River, on both sides of the border, the people of Mexican descent tell of these creatures. They don't call them *tecolotes*, or *búhos* that are other names for owls. When they say *lechuza*, they speak of an evil shape-shifting witch who can transform into an owl to wreak havoc on its enemies."

"Father, can such a thing be?"

"My brethren who work with the Choctaw Indians of Northern Texas and Oklahoma tell me that among the Choctaw there is a belief of a creature they call the *witch-owl*. Only the name is different," the padre responded.

"Then it is true?"

"I cannot say for sure, but even the Old Testament tells of these things. King Nebuchadnezzar in the

Book of Daniel, for his arrogance, was transformed into a bull..."

"Father, how does one protect himself from such things?"

The padre said, "I shall give you a special blessing..."

When Roberto got home, he was upset to find three more dead cardinals in his backyard. Perhaps he would get a dog to keep Pingo out of his backyard. After gathering the dead birds Roberto decided to wait until the day was cooler to bury them.

He got into his '49 GMC pickup truck and drove to town. Where could he get a dog? The big cities had pet stores, but it was too far to drive. He delivered mail, but he was at loss at who would have a dog to give away. Maybe Blanca Patricia at the feed store knew someone.

"Mr. Corona, back so soon?"

"Hello Blanca. I wanted to ask you if you knew someone who had a dog he wanted to give away."

"We mated Paquito. The puppies are due any day."

Lechuza

"Hmm, no Blanquita, I think I need a big dog, not a puppy. One big and mean enough to keep Pingo out of my backyard."

"Pingo is still giving you trouble?"

"Well something is killing the songbirds in my backyard."

"I'm sorry, Mr. Corona. If I hear of someone with a big dog to give away, I'll refer him to you."

"Thank you, Blanca."

Roberto decided to drive into Laredo to go see a movie and maybe go shopping at the Kress Department store. When he returned to his house, it was already after dark.

He went indoors and started turning on lights. In the kitchen he fixed some cold cereal and readied to go to bed. Suddenly he remembered. He still hadn't buried the dead Cardinals. He stared at his watch and sighed, realizing that he should bury the dead birds before going to bed.

From his tool shed in the backyard he retrieved a long-handled spade and he proceeded to dig a hole three feet deep. Soon his task was completed and after tapping the bird's grave with the back of his spade, packing the dirt tightly, he decided to check the birdfeeder for rice.

Lechuza

The moon was full and gave off enough light to see if the feeders had rice. Atop his ladder checking the first feeder, a dark shadow descended over him. He looked back in time to see a *lechuza* swooping down on him.

"*¡Tiene un ojo opaco y cara de mujer!*" he exclaimed, quickly jumping from the ladder. *The owl had one opaque eye and a woman's face!* Now the *lechuza* flew straight up and circled to make another pass.

Roberto landed on his feet and rolled on the ground to break his fall. As the *lechuza* came at him again, he grabbed his spade and swung. He swatted the big bird hard, hard enough to break the spade's handle in two. The *lechuza* tumbled to the ground leaving a wake of white feathers floating gently in the night air.

The following morning Roberto awoke early, rose out of bed and went to his kitchen to fix coffee. Out of his kitchen window he saw a bright red cardinal singing happily from the old *huisache* tree.

He poured a cup of freshly brewed coffee and stepped out onto the front porch.

Lechuza

It was a beautiful morning. The air was crisp and dry with just a hint of winter in the air. The Lechuza was no where to be found.

Tommy Martinez, the paperboy, was on his bicycle throwing newspapers. "*Hola* Tommy," Roberto called out a friendly greeting from his front porch.

"*Hola* Mr. Corona," Tommy said, "have you heard the news?"

"No, Tommy, I just woke up."

"Your neighbor, *Doña* Luz, broke her back."

"Broke her back?"

"*Sí*, Mr. Corona. My father, the Sheriff, says she must have fallen off her bed during the night."

"Well, is she alright?"

Trying to suppress a grin Tommy manages to say, "She is dead Mr. Corona. My father says, *¡sus culpas ha pagado*—she's paid for her sins!"

From a distance, one can still hear Pingo's mournful yowling as he calls out to his mistress.

Lechuza

Chapter 23

Far, Pharr From Heaven

October 23,1970 was one day away from my twenty-second birthday. It was approximately seven years after President John F. Kennedy was assassinated in Dallas, Texas, and a lifetime before the infamous, terrorist attack on the Twin-Towers that killed thousands of Americans in New York City.

I was attending classes part-time at Texas A & I University in Kingsville, Texas (later known as Texas A & M at Kingsville), and I worked full-time for the City of Kingsville as a police dispatcher.

I dated a girl from McAllen, Texas, so I spent a lot of my free time in the Lower Rio Grande Valley, a little over an hour's drive from Kingsville. The girl was a telephone operator and was one of the few persons I knew who had a telephone credit card. Practically all telephone calls were long distance then, and because she did have a card, it was not a surprise when her telephone call woke me up early in the morning.

205

Lechuza

I had worked the graveyard shift the night before, and I was sleeping in when her call came. I assumed that Connie was calling to wish me an early happy birthday, but the tone of her voice was not festive. She sounded downcast.

"What's wrong," I asked?

"Have you heard the News?"

"No, I was sleeping, what News?"

The Incident

"An airplane crashed into Our Lady of San Juan Church," she practically whimpered.

Connie was a devoted Roman Catholic and a frequent church goer. I, not so much. None-the-less, I was distressed by the news.

"Are many people hurt," I managed to ask?

"Too early to tell, we hope not, but the pilot is dead."

I jumped out of bed and assured Connie that I was on my way.

Lechuza

Even though Connie lived in McAllen, all the towns in the area—Edinburg, Pharr, San Juan, and McAllen had practically merged. It was difficult to tell where one town ended and the other one began. And we both had many mutual friends living in the Valley who attended Mass at the Basilica of Our Lady of San Juan del Valle.

As a teen, my family had made pilgrimages to the Shrine of Our Lady of San Juan, from Hebbronville, Texas, which is not in the Valley, but more than a hundred miles north.

San Juan del Valle—the Shrine, is in the City of San Juan, as the name implies.

I was groggy, but the shocking news jarred me into awareness. I was shocked, outraged, saddened, and concerned for my friends in the area, a predominately Catholic Mexican American community. Our Lady of San Juan del Valle united us into one common faith-community, as a people of dual languages, Spanish and English, and as Roman Catholics.

Connie had made it sound as if the airplane had deliberately crashed into the Church. This was difficult to comprehend. By and large, the Valley was a friendly place where Catholics and non-Catholics worked well together and did not let belief differences come between them. In reality, more rivalry existed about which football teams for which to cheer, or which beer was better, Budweiser or Schlitz beer. The Valley was a nice place to live.

Springtime in the Valley, when all the citrus orchards were in bloom, was beautiful. The air was permeated with the sweet odor of citrus blossoms. It is so hard to believe now, that we took all that for granted back then.

People who owned small acreage of citrus close to the city limits, supplemented their income by renting trailer spaces between the rows of citrus to the winter Texans. These trailer parks were called *tin-can-jungles*, and these visitors escaping harsh winters in the northern states were fondly referred to as *snowbirds*. Small wonder that the Rio Grande Valley of Texas came to be known as *The Magic Rio Grande Valley*.

And now a major tragedy had taken place in this magical place that in a split-second destroyed a most beloved Roman Catholic Shrine dedicated to Mother Mary, the Mother of Jesus Christ. I do not know what I expected to do when I got there, except pickup Connie, go to the site of the tragedy, and shed a tear or two.

I stopped by the corner convenience store in Kingsville for a large cup of black coffee, no sugar, and a light snack for the road. Lou Ann, the cashier, asked me if I had heard what had happened in the Valley?

I nodded adding, "I'm on my way there now, Lou Ann."

I drove a silver, 1963 rag-top, Triumph two-seat sports car then, that featured a primitive cable cruise control. I set the cruise speed as close to the maximum legal speed limit as it permitted, and I arrived at Connie's house in McAllen about an hour-and-a-half later. I said hello to her sister and hobnobbed with her parents briefly before we both got into my car and drove to the scene of the plane crash.

The Airplane

There were still a lot of people at the scene, behind the yellow tape, and firemen walked around the debris field sifting through the ashes. On what was left of the roof of the church I observed the skeletonized remains of what I mistakenly thought was a high-wing Cessna, single-engine airplane, possibly a Cessna 150 or 152.

Subsequent news reports revealed that the airplane was actually a rented Piper Cherokee 180, a single-engine, four-seat airplane. These airplanes have a fuel capacity of 50 gallons in two wing tanks. A veritable flying missile. Could this be the reason the pilot selected this particular model to rent? Most pilots I know seem to prefer the Cessna with their high-wing design. They say that it is easier to land a high wing Cessna on a highway during an emergency because the wing will go over road signs. Not so with the Piper and its under-the-fuselage wing design.

Also, the Cessna 152 carries less fuel than the Piper, and some Cessna 152s are rated to fly on automobile gasoline, rather than the more expensive and volatile aviation fuel. Was this a consideration for the pilot when he rented this airplane, choosing one capable of causing more death, mayhem, and destruction? There is no way to know since the pilot was the only fatality in the crash.

The Pilot

The pilot was approximately fifty years of age. He was a former schoolteacher who resigned his teaching post with the Pharr-San Juan-Alamo school district the previous spring.

Pilot Frank B. Alexander was considered an authority in teaching migrant children. Alexander

210

also was a flight instructor. Alexander's body was recovered from the destroyed structures, still strapped to the pilot's seat when recovered.

Charles Wardroup was in the control tower at Miller International Airport in McAllen. Wardroup stated that a call was received from a pilot later identified as Alexander, ordering the fire department to evacuate all Roman Catholic and Methodist Churches between Hidalgo, Edinburg, Weslaco, and McAllen, all in the lower Rio Grande Valley. When asked the reason for this strange order, the pilot simply replied: "Because of a serious plot."

Was it possible that the pilot was still debating which Church to destroy? And why even mention Methodist Churches if his ire was to be directed at the Shrine of Our Lady of San Juan? It would seem that he was trying for misdirection, except that only minutes later his plane crashed into the Shrine at the point where the cafeteria and the Church joined, the plane and buildings erupted into flames.

A spokesman for the McAllen Police Department stated: There was no time to evacuate anyone. As we were picking up the phones and dialing, the plane crashed.

The Church and cafeteria were destroyed and only the steel girders remained. Reverend E. A.

Ballard, Chancellor of the Brownsville Diocese of
which the Church complex is a part of, estimated
the loss at $1.5 million. The Church is part of a
complex which include St. John's Catholic School
and a retreat house. The school is across the
street at the rear of the Church; however, the
children eat in the cafeteria.

The Shrine of the Virgin of San Juan is well
known to Roman Catholics in Northern Mexico
and in Texas. The white church of stone and brick
was about the height of a two-story building. The
steeple towered some four or five stories high, and
the Church itself could accommodate about 800
worshippers.

Reverend Ronald Anderson, Vice Chancellor of the
Diocese stated, "We first heard an explosion and
we all rushed out."

The spokesman for the aviation company which
rented the plane to Alexander stated that he was
an instructor-pilot who often rented their planes.
Alexander rented the plane about 11:00 a.m. that
morning and said that he planned to fly around in
the local area. Employees of the Airplane rental
stated that they noticed nothing unusual about
Alexander's mannerisms that morning.

Sister Margaret, principal of St. John's Catholic
School, 50 yards from the Church, said she saw
the airplane strike the Church. "I saw the plane

coming," Sister Margaret said, "It was making all sorts of noise and shaking... Suddenly it hit the top of the Church. I saw the fire burst out and I thought, 'Oh, the children.' I ran to the cafeteria to get them out."

Mrs. Romelia de la Rosa, a teacher's aide who was in the cafeteria with about 200 children said, "We only heard a noise. A father came in and said the Church was on fire and to get the children out of there."

The children left their lunch half-finished. Classes were immediately dismissed for the day.

Mario Reyes, 11, a sixth grader who was in the school cafeteria, stated: "We heard the plane, then the explosion. I looked over to the Church and saw a lot of smoke."

A huge crowd and traffic jammed the area as firemen from several Valley towns fought the blaze unsuccessfully. A wing and part of the fuselage lodged between the Church and cafeteria. Sheriff Claudio Castaneda said that Department of Public Safety officers searched the still burning wreckage of the plane but did not locate the pilot right away.

Superintendent Dean Skiles of the Pharr-San Juan-Alamo schools said Alexander, a resident of San Juan, resigned as a teacher April 28, effective at the end of the last school year.

213

Lechuza

Justice of the Peace, Dario Garcia of McAllen, said an autopsy had been request by the Federal Aviation Agency (on Pilot Alexander's body).

(*Corpus Christi Caller-Times Texas October 24, 1979.)

The Aftermath

By the Grace of God, and the intercession of the Holy Mother herself, none of the thirty Priests, two-hundred children, Religious Sisters and Catechists present in the Church and in the cafeteria that day, were killed or injured. To this very day his motives remain unknown, but in Christian charity we can only pray that God, in His infinite mercy, may deem that Frank B. Alexander Rest in Peace.

Thanks to the quick actions of Father Patricio Dominguez, OMI, (Oblates of Mary Immaculata), a missionary Priest, along with the help of Sacristan Pedro Rodriguez, the statue of Our Lady of San Juan del Valle was carried to safety.

Father Ron Anderson, a Diocesan Priest, carried the Blessed Sacrament off before the altar was engulfed in flames. Sister Margaret, the principal of St. John's Catholic School, as well as the

unknown father (a parent or perhaps a Priest?)
who rushed to the aid of the 200 children in the
cafeteria and helped teacher's aide Mrs. Romelia
de la Rosa evacuate the cafeteria. All three
displayed uncommon valor rushing into harm's
way to rescue the children from a burning
building. The quick action of these three brave
souls indubitably was the reason that none of the
children suffered injuries or death, that dark
October day in 1970.

Eventually the Shrine, Church and cafeteria were
rebuilt. I have returned to the Basilica of Our Lady
of San Juan del Valle several times since that day
in 1970. Once was during the mid-1980's when
my wife, family and I still resided in Bruni, TX.
A visiting Priest from Mexico to Our Lady of
Guadalupe Parish Church in Hebbronville, Texas
wanted to visit the Shrine of Our Lady of San
Juan del Valle. As an architect, he was interested
in viewing the architecture of the new Church.

Our Pastor, Fr. Benjamin Orozco, OFM, asked me
if I could take the visiting Priest to the San Juan
Shrine. I agreed to chauffer the visiting Priest to
the Shrine. We were there and back the same day.

More recently in 2018, a friend of mine wanted to
go see Our Lady of San Juan del Valle. She and

her niece did not want to go alone and so I was invited. I am happy that I was able to accompany them.

I am also pleased to say that Our Lady of San Juan del Valle is as beautiful as ever. Not even the slightest singe mark anywhere. To one such as I, who viewed the burned-out airplane and the burned down edifices, it is nothing less than a miracle.

Lechuza

Chapter 24

Phantom Encounter in Falfurrias

Roberto Salinas, Jr. was excited to share this true tale about his father with me.

"My Dad, Roberto Salinas Sr., was a truck driver. His route took him all over South Texas making deliveries of fresh milk. That memorable night, when my father left our home in Edinburg, Texas, a hard-driving rain had already begun to fall. Dad reported that the weather only became worse as he drove north on US Highway 281 toward Falfurrias, Texas. As Dad rolled into the City of Falfurrias, he slowed down considerably due to the inclement weather. Even on their fastest setting the windshield wipers could barely clear the rain away.

As he approached the intersection of US-281 and SH-285, Dad noticed a hitchhiker soliciting a ride by the side of Highway 281. Dad considered picking him up but thought better of it and continued driving. Something seemed unnatural about this person. Perhaps it was the way the shadows seem to shroud him, or perhaps it was the way he stood, shoulders hunched, hat pulled down obscuring his features in the driving rain.

Lechuza

Dad felt badly about leaving the man in the pouring rain but the very sight of him made Dad uneasy.

As Dad slowed down to negotiate a right turn onto State Highway 285, luck was with him. His traffic light remained green and he did not have to stop at all to make that right turn. Dad had only driven some two blocks east on SH-285 when he sensed a presence in the cab of his truck. Out of his peripheral vision Dad noticed the strange hitchhiker now sitting beside him in the passenger side of his truck.

As inconspicuously as possible Dad reached with his left hand for the tire billy stored in the storage well of the driver's side door. With the billy secure in his left hand, Dad turned to face the stranger. He was soaking wet and his face was still swathed in shadows. The stranger looked straight ahead and totally ignored Dad as he attempted to engage him in polite conversation.

Dad asked him when he had gotten into the cab, but the stranger just stared ahead and said nothing. Dad continued driving toward the next town which was Riviera, Texas. During this tense 30-minute drive to Rivera, the strange man never spoke. He never even responded to Dad's friendly conversation.

Lechuza

Dad made his mind up to stop in Riviera and, if necessary, force the unwanted hitchhiker to get out there. Determined to reach Riviera and be rid of this unwanted rider, Dad concentrated on his driving on the rain-slick road. As Riviera came into sight, Dad slowed his truck down and came to a complete stop right at the railroad tracks just prior to SH-77. Here Dad turned to face the hitchhiker, "Okay," Dad started, "This is where you get off..." His voice trailed off.

The stranger was no longer there. Dad got off and walked all around his truck. No one was anywhere to be seen. Now Dad opened the passenger side cab door of his truck. The passenger side seat and floorboard were soaking wet, but the dark stranger was nowhere to be seen. He had vanished as mysteriously as he had appeared."

The End

Lechuza

Lechuza

Acknowledgements

1) Officer Rick Petrie
2) Officer Bob Jamison
3) Officer Moss Clark
4) Officer Frank Doyle
5) Officer Ron Holden
6) Officer Mike Hudson
7) Sgt. Calvin Smith
8) Officer Roy Whittaker
9) Officer Jaime Falcon
10) Officer Steve Long
11) Officer Mark Harrington
12) Officer Craig Lee
13) Officer Frank Dyson
14) Officer Brad Smith
15) Lt. Ignacio García
16) Sgt. Leroy Davis
17) Officer Ben Lillard
18) Officer Phillip Suarez
19) Officer James Porter
20) Officer David Hall
21) Officer Luther Odom
22) Officer Elias Sonny Martinez
23) Officer Lina Stevenson
24) Officer Goree Anderson
25) Officer Wendy Stewart Burkes

Also, two other police officers who worked for different departments but who were close to the Metro Police:

Harris County Pct. 4 Warrant-Deputy Constable
Gumaro *Gumby* Barrera

and

Captain (retired) City of Edinburg Police
Department
Roberto Salinas

A special thank you, to Metro Senior Police Officer Raymond Williams. Officer Williams has kept an accurate record of the Metro Police Officers who have perished since 1996. Without this record I would not have easily been able to compile this list of deceased officers for this dedication.

Also, thank you Metro Police Dispatcher Lisa Barrera who apprised me of the list Senior Officer Raymond Williams was maintaining of the deceased Officers. Thank you also, Lisa, for putting me in touch with Officer Williams.

Thank you, Compadre and Comadre Roel and Bebe Cremar, and mom-in-law Amelia Garza, for your contributions to this collection of *Cuentos Viejos*. Also, thank you Roberto Salinas, my old friend, and fellow police officer for you your contributions to this collection. Thank all of you for your friendship.

Lechuza

Lechuza

CPSIA information can be obtained
at www.ICGtesting.com
Printed in the USA
LVHW082323090820
662774LV00008B/1104